Lily's Story

A Puppy Tale

Also by
W. Bruce Cameron

Lily's Story

A Puppy Tale

WITHDRAWN

W. Bruce Cameron

Illustrations by

Richard Cowdrey

STARSCAPE

A Tom Doherty Associates Book
New York

LILY'S STORY

Copyright © 2019 by W. Bruce Cameron

Reading and Activity Guide copyright © 2019 by Tor Books
Illustrations © 2019 by Richard Cowdrey

A Starscape Book
Published by Tom Doherty Associates
120 Broadway
New York, NY 10271

www.tor-forge.com

The Library of Congress Cataloging-in-Publication Data is available
upon request.

ISBN 978-1-250-21351-8 (hardcover)
ISBN 978-1-250-21350-1 (ebook)

Our books may be purchased in bulk for promotional, educational, or business use.
Please contact your local bookseller or the Macmillan Corporate and Premium
Sales Department at 1-800-221-7945, extension 5442, or by email
at MacmillanSpecialMarkets@macmillan.com.

First Edition: October 2019

Printed in the United States of America

0 9 8 7 6 5 4 3 2 1

For Sheri Kelton,
who appeared at exactly the moment I
needed her and has been there providing
guidance, assistance, wisdom, and
professional boxing management
ever since.
Couldn't do this without you, Sheri.

Lily's Story

A Puppy Tale

1

I had a mother and no sisters and too many brothers.

We all lived inside a clean, warm kennel. Our kennel had three walls that I couldn't see through and one that I could. The one I could see through was made of thin wires twisted together. I could glimpse what was on the other side, but I couldn't squeeze through the gaps in the wires.

None of us could, though we tried. We knew there were things out there to smell and taste and chew, more things than we could find inside our kennel home.

Above us was a high ceiling and, in the back of our pen, a soft dog bed. That was where I would sleep with my mother dog, usually with one or more brothers draped across me.

What I saw through the wire, directly across from us, was another kennel just like ours, but empty. I could smell and hear other animals outside our kennels—there were dogs who barked and dogs who didn't and strange-smelling animals who were not dogs and made mewing sounds. Other not-dogs chattered or hissed. But I never saw any of these animals, and they didn't come into the kennel with us.

We had not always lived here. I faintly remembered a different place with different smells. There, I was cold. In the kennel, I was not.

When we lived in the cold place, my only meals had been milk from my mother. Soon after arriving at the kennel, though, I ate different food. The wall that I could see through had a gate that would swing open, and then a woman would come in with soft mush in a bowl.

My mother would greet this woman and lick her hands while her tail wagged happily, so I knew the lady was nice. She was safe. I could trust her. My brothers certainly trusted her; they rushed to her and jumped up toward her face and bit at her hair. I usually hung back so I wouldn't be trampled. But I liked her just the same.

If I didn't have all these brothers, I could have shown

the woman how much I liked her. Also how much I liked her food—which was very much.

But I didn't always get to eat as much of that food as I wanted.

That was because I had too many brothers. I thought about this fact a *lot,* especially when one of them was jumping on me or blocking me from where I wanted to go.

The largest brother was white with gray splotches like me. Another was black with a white tip to his tail, and the third was brown all over. They all had soft ears and big paws and busy tails. So did I. But they were all bigger than I was. A lot bigger, which seemed to lead them to believe they could push me around.

It had always been hard for me to find a place to feed on my mother's milk, because a brother or two would try to shoulder me aside. In the kennel, it was hard for me to gobble up enough meaty mush from the bowl, because my brothers wanted to get there first, and I couldn't always shove my way in.

My brothers stepped on my face when we played. They slept on top of me until I felt flat. They were louder and quicker and rougher than I was, and when we wrestled, I always ended up on the bottom of the pile.

Sometimes I thought life would just be easier without *any* brothers.

If a brother bit my tail or fell down on my head or

stuck a paw in my eye, I yipped or squealed. Then my mother would come to find me. She'd pick me up by the back of my neck. Sometimes, I could feel the gentle bite of my mother's teeth on the nape of my neck before her mouth was even there, feel her warm breath, all in my imagination.

My mother would carry me to the back of our kennel, where our bed was made of soft pillows on the floor. There she'd lie down with me. Her body usually curled into a circle with me at the center.

I loved lying with my mother. She was a girl dog, just like me. I could smell it. We were the only two girls in our kennel. I thought that was why she loved me best.

At least, I hoped she did.

Sometimes, when I was curled up with my mother, I watched people walk by our kennel. That was pretty much all there was to see unless I wanted to look at my brothers. Most of the people would stride busily past, going in one direction or another.

But one day, the woman who brought us food stopped at our kennel. I picked up my head with interest, because she had other people with her! Smaller people who moved more quickly and a bit more clumsily than she did.

Young humans. Children.

My nose twitched. I could smell two boys and a girl.

The boys were bigger; the girl was smaller. Just like *my* family!

I glanced over at my brothers. They weren't paying any attention. As usual, they were piled up in a heap by a wall of the kennel. Brown-Brother was chewing on a toy. Biggest-Brother was chewing on Brown-Brother's leg. White-Tail-Brother was getting ready to jump on Biggest-Brother's head.

"Oh!" said the girl on the other side of the wire. It was a long, drawn-out sound that had both happiness and longing in it. "Oh, puppies!"

I got up and shook myself and scampered forward to investigate.

The girl knelt down and stuck her fingers through the wire. I sniffed at them. They smelled wonderful. I could pick up the scent of salty sweat and soft skin and dirt and something sticky and sweet. She giggled when I started licking. I wagged at the giggles.

Then all my brothers barreled into me. Before I knew it, I was buried under wagging, panting, yipping puppies.

"Get out of the way, Maggie Rose!" I heard someone say.

I wiggled, backing up. When I pulled my head out of the pile of brothers, I saw that the girl was no longer on her knees by the wire. The boys had pushed her to one side so that they could kneel down and put their own fingers into our kennel and laugh as my siblings licked and nibbled and squealed for attention.

I was pretty sure that the girl was the sister and that the bigger boys were her brothers. I could tell by their scents. The way my littermates smelled like me, she smelled like the two boys. Besides, I knew that pushing and shoving was exactly how brothers behaved.

They all had the same brown hair, but the girl's curled at her shoulders, and the boys both had hair that ended close to their heads. The taller one's hair was neatly pushed to one side, while the younger boy had hair that stuck out all over.

"Move over, Craig!" the younger boy said, poking the larger one with his elbow.

"Don't shove, Bryan!" the bigger one answered, pushing back. His breath had an odor on it that I would soon learn came from peanut butter. It was very attractive. I really wanted to know more about peanut butter.

The girl—Maggie Rose?—looked up at the woman. "Mom? Why is the girl puppy so small?" she asked.

"She's the runt of the litter," the woman, Mom, answered. "It happens, honey. One puppy's born small, and then it's hard for her to get her fair share of food or milk, so she doesn't grow as quickly as the others."

The younger boy looked up from where he was letting White-Tail-Brother chew on his fingers.

"Runt—that's what we need to call you, Maggie Rose," he said with a laugh.

I sat and looked at the girl and the mother, high over my brothers' heads. I could see the girl's shoulders and head droop a little at her brother's words.

"Bryan, that's enough," Mom told him sternly. "Make some room for me." Mom reached over to open the gate in the wire wall.

As soon as the gate swung open, my brothers rushed into the hallway, piling onto the boys, jumping up to lick their faces and bite their hands. Craig and Bryan flopped down on the floor, laughing, and my brothers climbed over them just as they did to our mother when they wanted to play.

I stayed inside the kennel. I would have liked to smell and taste these new people close up and to find out if they had any food anywhere. But I knew about this kind of play. It always ended up with me getting squashed and stepped on.

"Oh, puppy, it's okay," Maggie Rose called softly. She sat down and held out her hands. "You can come. Come and see me."

I liked her voice. I wanted to lick her hands some more. Carefully, I stepped around the wrestling boys and brothers and bounded over to Maggie Rose's lap.

She didn't make any quick movements. She touched me gently. Her hands tasted just as good as before. I stuck my nose into the crease under her chin, where her skin was sweaty and delicious.

She giggled. "That tickles!" she said.

"I'm going to name this one Gunner!" declared Bryan, holding up White-Tail-Brother so that his legs paddled in the air.

"This one's Butch!" said Craig, scratching Biggest-Brother's belly.

"How about Rodeo for the brown one?" Bryan said.

"No way. Zev! His name should be Zev!"

"I'm going to name this one Lily," Maggie Rose said. She put an arm around me, and I curled up into a ball in her lap. It felt as cozy as sleeping with my mother.

"No way," Craig said. "How about . . . Katie?"

"How come I don't get to name a puppy?" the girl, Maggie Rose, complained.

"Because you're a runt!" Bryan hooted.

"I'm not going to ask you again, Bryan," Mom warned. "Maggie Rose, of course you can name that puppy if you want."

"Then I'm naming her Lily," Maggie Rose said.

"Stupid name," Craig muttered.

"Why would anybody name a dog after a flower?" Bryan jeered. "She's not even completely white. Lilies are 100 percent white."

"It's my favorite flower," Maggie Rose replied. Her voice was quiet but stubborn. "I'm naming her Lily."

Mom had walked away and was standing a few yards down the hallway, talking to a tall woman I had seen before. The woman had short black hair and boots on her feet. "Okay, boys, time to go," Mom called.

"Aw, Mom," Craig groaned. "We just got here."

"Soccer practice waits for no man, Craig. Or boy. Put the puppies back in the kennel."

"Mom, can I stay?" Maggie Rose pleaded. "I don't want to go to their soccer practice."

"They might get confused and use you as a ball, runt!" Bryan teased her. He kept his voice low, and I didn't think Mom could hear him.

Mom and the tall woman talked some more. "It's fine; I'll keep an eye on her," the tall woman agreed.

"Okay, Maggie Rose, you can stay," Mom called over. "Amelia's in charge. Help out and do what she tells you."

Maggie Rose grinned. She hugged me close to her face, which gave me a chance to push my head into her brown hair and sniff up the scents hiding in it.

The human brothers left. My dog brothers charged over to Maggie Rose, climbing into her lap, lapping at her face. Maggie Rose curled an arm around me to protect me.

She stood up, still holding me tightly. Brothers plopped off her lap and onto the floor. Maggie Rose herded them back to the kennel and shut the door on them.

They yipped and barked and put their paws up on the door. My mother, still lying at the back of the kennel, picked up her head and watched alertly, but she made no movements.

"I'm going to take you on an adventure, Lily," Maggie Rose said to me.

I liked her smell. I liked her voice. I liked her hands. But I didn't know where she was taking me as she carried me away from my kennel, away from my mother and brothers. Where were we going?

2

As Maggie Rose carried me out into the room, I saw that there were lots of kennels like the one where I lived with my mother and brothers. In some of them, there were dogs. I was excited to see them, because I'd had their scents in my nose for some time!

"You're a sweet puppy, Lily. You're so calm," Maggie Rose told me. "I'm going to be a veterinarian when I grow up so I can help dogs like you." I had no idea what the talking was all about, but I was learning to love the soft, high sound of her voice. "Okay, you ready? Time to meet new friends, Lily."

One kennel held a large black dog with shaggy fur

that nearly completely covered his eyes. "That's Poppy! Hi, Poppy! Poppy just arrived here at the shelter."

Poppy watched Maggie Rose pass but didn't react. In the next kennel, a small white dog, a boy, was asleep in his bed. A brown dog, a girl, snorted at us. She had tight, short fur, a white chest, and a pushed-in face. Her tail was a tiny brown stub that quivered as if she were wagging it.

Maggie Rose paused by the next pen, and a dog inside came wagging to the wire gate. He was big and sleek and black, with a brown face and white around his muzzle. Maggie Rose held me down so that I could touch noses with him through the wire.

He was male like my brothers! But older than they were, even older than my mother. I had never known that there could be male dogs as big and old as this.

"Hi, Brewster! This is Brewster, Lily." Maggie Rose told me. "His family had to move, and they couldn't take care of him anymore. He's an older dog, and he's been here for a long time, and Mom says he's safe for me to talk to because he's been evaluated. That means Mom and Amelia have tested his behavior. We're going to find him a new family. That's what we do, Lily. We find families for animals who don't have homes. Like you!"

I wiggled around to lick her nose.

She giggled and carried me on.

"You came here when your eyes were barely open. You were a newborn, and you and your mommy dog lived with a man who decided he couldn't take care of you, so he brought you and your brothers here. My mom started working for this rescue last year. She's the boss. We mostly save dogs and cats, but we've had goats and turtles and even some chickens!"

The big room that we were in changed as we left the old dog behind us. In this part, there were no long, narrow kennels. Along a wall, there were smaller cages, stacked one on top of the other, each made of wires and each with a door.

In the first cage, an animal about my size hesitated in the back corner of its pen. I stared. Whatever this was, it wasn't a dog! I recognized its odor as one of the not-dogs I'd been smelling all this time. "This is Oscar," Maggie Rose told me. "It's okay, Oscar. Lily won't hurt you. Come on up and say hi." She crouched down beside the gate.

Slowly the animal approached. He had sleek gray fur and wide yellow eyes and triangular ears that stood straight up on his head. I'd never seen ears like that! My own ears flopped down beside my face like my mother's and my brothers'.

Maggie Rose tucked me under one arm and stuck the fingers of her other hand through the wire. Oscar sniffed her. I thought he'd lick her fingers, which seemed like the proper thing to do, but instead he rubbed his face on them and made a low, rumbly noise. How strange!

"This is your first cat, isn't he, Lily?" Maggie Rose asked me. "Oscar loves people. Most strays are scared, but he's not. He's going to get adopted soon, I bet. Mom says he just has to be neutered first. That's so he can't make any babies. I love kittens, but there are already too many running loose in the world, Mom says. Okay, you can say hi to the cat, but be nice. See the cat, Lily?"

Cat. The not-dog was a cat. Maggie Rose held me closer to the wire, and I inhaled Oscar's smell eagerly. It was so interesting to meet an animal who wasn't a dog! Oscar sniffed at me, too, and then he retreated back inside the cage, his tail up high and quivering nervously.

"Oscar isn't sure about dogs, even a little one like you," Maggie Rose said. She stood back up. "Come on, Lily."

In another cage, two more cats stared at me blankly. They didn't come to sniff me, but maybe that was just how cats were. Someday they'd be ready to be friends with me, I was sure about that. I pictured wrestling with them and wagged at the thought. They were close to my size. Wrestling with them would be much fairer than wrestling with my brothers.

Maggie Rose picked me up so that I could see into the next cage. I thought at first I was looking at another cat. The animal inside moved in the same kind of smooth, slinky way. But he had a longer body and shorter legs than Oscar did. He didn't smell like Oscar, either. He smelled fiercer, somehow. Wilder.

Another kind of not-dog!

Unlike the two cats in the previous cage, this animal came right up to the wire to stretch his neck up high and touch his small nose to mine. He had round black eyes that gleamed in the dim light and a black mask that covered half of his brown face. His whiskers tickled my nose!

"Hi, Freddie!" Maggie Rose said. "Freddie's not scared of anything, Lily. He's a ferret. He's just staying with us for the summer. In the fall, he's going back to Craig's school. Craig will be in tenth grade. Bryan's in seventh. Anyway, Craig's school is where Freddie lives, in the science lab. He's got a big pen with ladders to climb and a hammock to sleep in, Craig says. Do you like the ferret, Lily? Do you think you could be friends with a ferret?"

I could see that Freddie had very strong white teeth underneath his twitching nose. He was interested in me and seemed to want to play. A ferret was like a friendly version of a cat.

"Mom says ferrets aren't really pets, and they should

be out living in the wild. But Freddie's never lived out-side, and he's too old to learn, so it's a good thing the science teacher takes care of him," Maggie Rose told me. "If we tried to set him free now, a coyote or a wild-cat could get him."

I wondered what all her talking meant. Was she say-ing that she was going to put me in the cage or that she was going to let Freddie come out to play? Either of those would be fine with me.

But it seemed that Maggie Rose had no intention of opening the cage door. I had no idea why. She was con-tent to just hold me up to the wires so I could examine the ferret.

Freddie seemed to figure out the same thing—that he wouldn't be coming out to play. Bored with just touching noses, he turned his back and dashed away, more quickly than I could run. He scrambled up a box and dived into a hole on the top. Moments later, his head poked out, and he looked at Maggie Rose and me before pulling his head back in.

"I guess Freddie doesn't want company right now," Maggie Rose said and carried me on.

I was very disappointed that we were leaving with-out any play. Perhaps I should have done something to let Maggie Rose know how much I wanted to wrestle with the ferret.

The next kennel she carried me to had yet another

new kind of animal! I was amazed. Before today, I had known that there were boy dogs and girl dogs, big dogs and small ones. And of course, people, too. Now I knew the smell and sight of cats and ferrets and—what was this thing?

It was smaller than Oscar, so it wasn't a cat. It had a face a bit like Freddie's, though its body was not as stretched out. This animal was stockier and rounder. It had a white chest and black eyes, and it had ears like a cat. Its tail was a huge, puffy thing that seemed to float up in the air behind its back, quivering and twitching with each movement.

It had one funny leg, all wrapped in something white that looked like cloth but that clunked loudly against the floor of the kennel. I'd never seen a leg like that!

Even with that funny leg, the creature moved quickly in little darting movements that were very exciting to watch. I squirmed until Maggie Rose put me down, and then I scratched at the gate and whined a little.

The gate was strange to touch; there was something smooth and clear over the wire so that my paw could not get inside. I couldn't really smell through it, either.

I wanted this little animal to come out or to let me in. I wanted to chase it. It needed to be chased!

I looked up expectantly at the girl, who was smiling down at me. I already knew that opening doors was something only people do—all dogs can do is sit and wait. So I sat and waited for Maggie Rose to open the door and let the quick, jerky creature out.

I knew as soon as she did, we would have a lot of fun!

3

Maggie Rose didn't seem to understand that I wanted to wrestle with this new and interesting not-dog. She hadn't understood that I wanted to play with Freddie, either. To make things clearer to her, I pawed helpfully at the smooth door again.

"No, Lily, Sammy can't come out," Maggie Rose said, laughing. "We're not supposed to play with him or touch him at all. He's a squirrel. He's not a pet. That's why his cage is glass, the kind of glass where we can see him but he can't see us. We're just taking care of him until his leg is better, and then he'll go back to the park. He can't get used to people feeding him or petting him or dogs playing with him, or he won't be safe in the wild, see? My dad rescued him. He's a game warden. He found Sammy caught in an illegal trap, and he even arrested the men who put the trap out!"

The animal was moving in such a tantalizing manner—quick little hops, its head making sudden jerky motions. I knew it must want to play Chase Me! I peered up at Maggie Rose and whined a little. I was wagging my tail so hard it thumped against my rump. Why didn't she understand? I needed her to open up the gate!

"Better leave Sammy alone. Lily, come with me," Maggie Rose said. She scooped me up.

I was astounded that we were leaving *again*. Why show me these wonderful playmates if they were going to remain in their cages?

Oh, well. If I couldn't play Chase Me with Sammy, at least I was able to snuggle with Maggie Rose. I leaned into her, very content. It was as nice as pressing up against my mother's side—better, even, because there was no risk of a couple of brothers stampeding up and crushing me.

Maggie Rose took me along a hallway lined with great big sacks, each one bigger than my mother. They smelled marvelous. I wiggled, ready to get down and sniff a sack close up and maybe get my teeth into the paper that covered it and pull hard enough to make whatever was inside spill out. But Maggie Rose held me close.

"No, Lily. You're too young to eat regular dog food," she told me. "And when you are old enough, your family will put it in a bowl for you."

We were approaching a door, and I heard a frightened yip from the other side, then another, and then another. I could tell there was an unhappy dog inside. She smelled older than I was, but younger than my mother. She was a girl, and her barks told me she was terrified.

Maggie Rose pushed the door open, and I saw that the tall woman with short black hair was holding a small dog on a table. Carefully, she wrapped white stuff around one of the dog's legs. I remembered that the woman's name was Amelia. The white lump on the dog's leg looked a lot like what Sammy had been dragging around.

Was that why we were all in this place, to get our legs wrapped up in white stuff? When was my turn? Could Amelia do my brothers first?

"Shut the door, Maggie Rose. I don't want this little girl to get loose," Amelia asked.

The frightened dog was trembling under Amelia's hands. She wasn't a puppy, but she was tiny, smaller than I was. Astounding! Every dog I had ever met before was bigger than I was. I'd just assumed I was the littlest puppy ever. But this female was the smallest dog imaginable! Amelia's hand could wrap around her entire rib cage.

The girl dog did not look like me. Instead of sleek, short fur in gray-and-white splotches, she had wiry black fur that stood out in all directions. The tufts were shaking with fright. I wagged. Why was she so frightened? Could I help?

"Is she a stray?" Maggie Rose asked.

"Nope, just lost. Someone found her on the streets and brought her in. She's got a bite on her leg; I guess she tangled with something, maybe a raccoon. A little Yorkie like this is no match for a big, aggressive raccoon."

"Will she be all right?" Maggie Rose asked.

"I think so," Amelia replied. "I cleaned the bite and gave her a stitch, and when her owner gets here, we'll send her home with antibiotics so the wound doesn't get infected. She should have been kept indoors or in a fenced yard, but people don't always do that. Still, the good news is that she's microchipped, so I already called her family. They'll be in to get her right away. Her name's Missy. There, there, sweetie, don't be scared. Your leg's all fixed."

"Good dog, Missy," Maggie Rose said.

"Poor thing is terrified," Amelia said sympathetically. "She's probably been shaking since she tussled with that raccoon. Why are you still so upset, Missy? You're safe. Here you go."

Amelia bent over to put the little dog, Missy, on the

floor. Missy sat down, hunched over, with her head low and her ears nearly flat against her skull. She had not been happy on the table, and now she was not happy to be down on the floor. She kept trembling.

"Go say hi, Lily," Maggie Rose told me. She set me down on the floor, too.

I studied Missy. She was not ready to play. If I bounded up to her as my bigger brothers did to me, it would only scare her more. She might even snap at me—she looked and smelled terrified enough to do it.

But there wasn't anything to be frightened of here. There was just Maggie Rose, who was gentle and nice, and Amelia, who was probably nice, too. I figured that out because Maggie Rose was talking to her and smiling. If Maggie Rose felt okay with Amelia, Amelia was okay by me.

I was the only other living thing in this room. And I wasn't scary. I was a puppy! I padded a little closer to Missy and then stopped and wagged my tail. This was how I wished my brothers would come close to me— slowly, calmly, so I could tell what they were going to do next.

I kept my head and ears up, but not so high that Missy would think I wanted to boss her around. I didn't want to boss her. I just wanted to play with her.

I moved a little closer.

Missy lowered her head a bit, studying me cautiously.

I stopped and waited.

Missy's ears lifted. That seemed friendly.

I crept closer and sniffed Missy all over. She still smelled scared, but not as scared as before. She smelled like Amelia's hands, and the white thing on her leg had a strange, sharp odor that I did not like.

But Missy's fur held a lot of very interesting scents. It smelled a bit like Maggie Rose's shoes, with hints of a place I had never been—someplace out there bigger than my kennel, someplace with dirt and air and wind and lots and lots of animals and people. One animal's odor in particular stood out in Missy's scruffy fur. It smelled like a not-dog and a little bit like Freddie—wild and untamed.

There were apparently very many not-dogs I needed to meet and play with. I was certainly learning a lot this day! It seemed as if the moment Maggie Rose picked me up, my world became much bigger, and my life changed.

Now Missy was sniffing me back, paying particular attention under my tail and between my rear legs. This was, I decided, how grown-up dogs greeted each other for the first time, with a polite sniff to the butt.

Missy shook herself. I shook, too, just to be friendly. Then Missy pushed at me a little with her nose. I pushed

back. I nibbled at her face. She shook herself and darted away. I flopped over on my back, legs in the air. Missy limped over and put her good paw across my belly.

I wiggled. She jumped away and bowed, front legs low, back legs high, tiny tail wiggling.

In a moment, we were wrestling. At last! I had finally found a new friend to wrestle with!

I knew to go easy with Missy, because her leg hurt her; I could tell by the way her scent changed when she put weight on it. But she did not let that stop her. It was fun playing with a smaller dog instead of three bigger brothers. Missy knew when to stop, too. When she bit down on my ear and I yipped, she backed off right away.

I liked Missy!

"Oh, look!" I heard Maggie Rose say. "Lily got Missy to play. She's not so scared now."

"Lily? Is that the puppy's name now? Good work, Lily." Amelia smiled. "A puppy can cheer anybody up."

"Did you see how gentle Lily was at first?" Maggie Rose asked.

"She must have sensed how afraid Missy was feeling," Amelia agreed. "Dogs can pick up on fear."

I heard a door open somewhere, and in a moment, a woman rushed into the room. A boy Maggie Rose's age followed behind her.

"Oh, Missy!" the woman wailed.

Missy stopped chewing on my face to bound over to

the woman's feet. The woman, tears flowing down her cheeks, snatched the little dog up and hugged her and held her close. "I was frantic! I just looked around and she was gone. It's been two days!" she cried.

Missy was not scared at all now. Missy was very, very happy.

This weeping woman was Missy's person, I realized with a jolt of understanding. That was why Missy was so overjoyed.

In that instant, I understood something new. My life here in this place with my mother and my big, heavy brothers was a good life, but it was not what a dog needed most. To be truly happy, a dog needed to be like Missy and have a person of her own.

Did I have a person? I looked up at Maggie Rose.

4

Maggie Rose caught me staring at her and smiled down at me, almost as if she knew what I was thinking. *Yes. Yes,* I realized. Of course Maggie Rose was my person. But did she know it? Did she know I was her dog?

I watched how Missy wouldn't stop kissing the crying woman. Missy had shown me the proper way to greet a new dog, and now she was showing me what to do if someone was your person. You showed how much you loved her, and then you were her dog.

That's what I would do. I would show Maggie Rose that I was her dog and that we belonged together forever.

The woman and Amelia talked, and Amelia gave the woman some papers and the woman gave them back. My girl, Maggie Rose, sat down on the floor to let me climb into her lap. Her hands stroked me, and I could feel the love flowing through them. I kissed her fingers the way Missy had kissed the crying lady's cheeks, letting my girl know that *yes, yes, yes*. Without words, I told her, *You are my person, Maggie Rose.*

The boy came over and knelt down beside us. "Can I pet him?" he asked. He had a soft, shy voice.

"She's a girl. Her name is Lily. Sure, you can pet her. She's really friendly," Maggie Rose said, and the boy reached out to rub my ears. Very nice.

"I'm glad you got your dog back," my girl told him.

"She's my mom's dog, really," the boy said. "But I'm glad, too."

The boy had stopped rubbing my ears, so I nosed his hand to get him to start it up again. When he did, I decided that if he wanted to live here with us, that would be okay by me. Maggie Rose was still my person, of course, but he could be a friend. "What kind is your dog?" he asked.

"Lily's not really mine," Maggie Rose said. Her voice sounded a little wistful, and I wondered why. I had a girl, and she had a puppy. I could think of no reason to be sad. "She's waiting for adoption. Her mom and brothers, too. We don't know what kind of dog the father was. The mom's a pit bull mix."

"She's cute," the boy said. "You can tell she really likes you."

Maggie Rose nodded. "She's a special dog."

"Time to go, Brandon," Wet Cheeks Woman called. Brandon jumped to his feet. As they were leaving, I looked up at Missy in the woman's arms. She looked back at me.

Missy was no longer afraid. I was happy that her fear was gone and grateful for the two things she had taught me: that dogs need to have a special person, and that when you first meet a dog, you should always sniff it in the butt.

Maggie Rose kept petting me, so I stayed in her lap, growing sleepier and sleepier.

"Going to take Lily back to her mom?" Amelia asked.

Maggie Rose didn't move.

"Maggie Rose? What's wrong, sweetie? Why do you have that expression?"

"I want her to be mine," my girl said, looking up at Amelia. "My own dog."

Amelia sighed. "Maggie Rose," she said gently. "We can't do that. We're a rescue organization. We save animals and find homes for them. We don't keep the animals ourselves. And there are all kinds of good reasons for that."

My girl held me close to her face. I was limp with sleepiness and didn't stir in her hands.

"It will work, Lily," Maggie Rose whispered to me. "I'll find a way for you to be my dog. I promise."

My girl carried me back to my kennel, but instead of putting me down so that my brothers could jump all over me, she carried me inside, shut the gate, and sat down with crossed legs on the floor. I curled up again in her lap and had a nice snooze there. I sort of knew that my brothers kept trying to hoist themselves over her knees and on top of me, but Maggie Rose kept them off. After a while, they stopped trying, and I supposed they were sleeping as well.

When I woke up, it was because I heard a door slam shut.

"Hi, Chelsea!" Amelia called out from somewhere else in the building. "Maggie Rose is back in the dog kennels."

I stretched and yawned in my girl's lap as the tall woman I'd seen before came down the row of pens, followed by Amelia. I remembered that Maggie Rose called the tall woman Mom.

My brothers were still all asleep, cuddled up against our mother.

"Time to say good-bye to the puppies," Mom told Maggie Rose. "The boys are waiting in the car. We need to go."

Maggie Rose didn't stir. She put her hands around me. It reminded me of the way my mother would curl her body around mine while I slept.

"I want to keep Lily," my girl declared. Her voice was soft. "I want to take her home with me."

"Oh no," Mom replied with a long sigh. "Maggie Rose, you know we can't do that."

Amelia had a sad smile on her face as she looked back and forth between Maggie Rose and Mom.

"I'll take care of her," Maggie Rose insisted. "She'll be my dog. I'll do all the work."

Mom sighed again, shaking her head. "For the summer, I'm sure you would. What about when you go to school in the fall? And I'm at work here? Who's going to look after Lily then?"

"I'll feed her and keep her clean and do everything before and after school." Maggie Rose gazed up at Mom imploringly. "Can't she come here with you? While you're working?" she asked.

Amelia looked at Mom. Mom looked at Amelia. I looked at them both.

"Listen, Maggie Rose," Mom said. "When someone who works in rescue takes an animal home and adopts it, it's called a foster failure. It sounds like a good thing, giving an animal a home, but it's not. Once someone has a pet, they usually stop fostering new animals. It's a big problem for a shelter like ours. So one of the first things I did when I started working here was to make a strict rule. Staff and volunteers can't adopt any animals from this shelter at all. It's better that way, believe me. Better for the animals and for us."

Now my girl was sad! I could feel it in her body. I snuggled closer, wondering what was troubling her. I wanted to help.

I had made Missy feel less scared. I ought to be able to make Maggie Rose feel less sad.

Amelia crouched down to look at Maggie Rose. "I can tell you really care about Lily, but your mom's right. Plus, we only have room for a few animals here. If Lily stays, then there's one less place for a rescue animal. That's not fair to all the animals who need us."

I rolled onto my back in Maggie Rose's lap and stuck my legs in the air. Now *this* should make anyone happy!

"But Lily could help," Maggie Rose insisted. The hope was draining out of her voice. "She likes the other animals. She helped with Missy."

Amelia sat back on her heels a little. "Well, that's true. Lily did help Missy calm down. But that doesn't change the facts, hon. We do the most good when we place animals into homes, and that's what we're going

to do with Lily. In another week or so, she'll be ready to leave her mother, and then we'll find her a good family who'll love her as much as you do."

My girl's mood was not improving. Time for some serious cheering up. I wriggled over onto my feet, put my front paws on Maggie Rose's chest, and tried to lick my girl on the chin. Instead of laughing, though, she just turned her head away.

"Maggie Rose," Mom said. "Put Lily down and come with me. You can visit her every day this week—right, Amelia? Even if I'm not here, you could watch my daughter?"

"Sure thing," Amelia agreed, standing back up. "I'll watch her. You always say it's important to get the puppies used to being with kids. Makes them better family dogs. Besides, Maggie Rose is a good worker."

My brothers were stirring, becoming alert as they realized there was still a girl in the kennel and that the door was open to the two women in the corridor.

"We're going home now, Maggie Rose." Mom patted my girl's shoulder, but her voice was firm. "Tell Lily good-bye."

"You can come help me as much as you want next week," Amelia said.

Mom and Amelia left the kennel and shut the gate behind them. My brothers rushed at the gate, milled around in confusion, and then turned their attentions to Maggie Rose in a stampede.

I could tell that my girl was still sad even though I was frantically licking her cheeks. She gave me a kiss before setting me down in the midst of the pack of jumping brothers. Then she slipped out the kennel door and stood for a moment, watching my littermates clamber all over me. What was going on? Why couldn't I kiss her and cuddle her into happiness?

"Don't worry, Lily," Maggie Rose whispered to me, sticking her fingers through the wires of the kennel. "I'll never let you go. You're going to stay with me."

I could hear good-bye in her voice. I licked Maggie Rose's fingers to tell her I was not done trying to make her happy, but she didn't seem to understand me. She stood and walked away.

I hurried over to my mother, my brothers on my heels, chewing on me as I went. Only the fact that they were also chewing on each other made it possible for me to duck into the protection of my mother's warm body.

I was ready for another nap after such an adventure outside my pen. Meeting other dogs and the cats and that long, funny ferret . . . playing with Missy . . . cuddling with Maggie Rose. It had all been very exciting, but it was time for a good long rest.

As I drifted off into sleep once more, I thought about what I now saw as my job—making Maggie Rose happy.

And I had a plan for that. Though there was not much I understood about, well, anything, I did know something about Maggie Rose.

5

What I knew about Maggie Rose, knew more than anything, was that she loved me. It was in the tender way her lips touched my face. It was in the warm, soft feel of her hands stroking me, in the way she stared into my eyes and cuddled me against her cheek. I was the puppy she loved, and if something was making her unhappy, I needed to fix it.

I just hoped she would give me a chance. Would I see her again soon? I thought I probably would.

Sure enough, Maggie Rose came back every day! I soon knew her scent and the sound of her footsteps, and I'd be waiting at the gate when she arrived, my tail wagging hard enough to make my entire butt wiggle. My girl would take me out and hug me and pet me. She'd sit on the floor and let me climb in her lap and lick her chin and sniff at her clothes, which were always full of the interesting odors she brought with her.

Most days, my girl arrived with Mom, but every now and then, a man came with them both. His name was Dad. He was taller than Mom and had shorter hair and a wide smile. He knew my name was Lily. "Hello, Lily," he would greet me. His voice was strong and deep.

I liked Dad. I especially liked his shoes. A complicated and marvelous smell clung to them, especially the soles. Maggie Rose's tennis shoes smelled a little like Dad's. Plus the laces were so good for pulling on.

I loved Maggie Rose's shoes. I loved Maggie Rose.

It wasn't long before I learned what made Maggie Rose's shoes—and Dad's, too—smell so good. A day came when Maggie Rose scooped me up in her hands. "Come on, Lily, we're taking you outside," she told me. Amelia and Mom picked my brothers up. They carried us down the hall to a door. My mother dog followed anxiously.

When they pushed open that door, I was astounded. A blast of warm air brought us so many new scents! I could see my brothers' noses twitching frantically and mine was doing the same. Giggling, Maggie Rose set me down in the short grass.

"I love it when they see the outside for the first time," Amelia said as she put White-Tail-Brother down beside me.

Outside! Outside was the best!

I wanted to do nothing but press my nose to the ground and inhale everything, but naturally, my brothers thought we were all out there to play Let's Climb on Lily. I dashed away from them, and Maggie Rose followed. Now we were all playing Chase Me! Maggie Rose was chasing me, and my brothers were chasing her while my mother sat and watched alertly. My girl was laughing and laughing. What a great day!

I wanted to stay in Outside forever, but after a while, we were all carried back to our pen. I slipped immediately into a nap, pressed up against my mother, dreaming of Outside.

I loved Outside nearly as much as I loved Maggie Rose. And she loved me. But all this love did not fix the problem. Deep inside, Maggie Rose was still sad, still wistful. I could tell that she was longing for something she could not have.

I could make her giggle, and she covered me with as many kisses as I gave her, but I couldn't take away this deep sadness. What Maggie Rose needed to do, I decided, was to come live with me here, in this place with all the dog kennels. She could sleep between my mother and me. I could work on keeping her giggling all day and night.

But Maggie Rose did not do this. She always went home at night, although she came back each day. Sometimes her big brothers came, too.

"Hey, runt. Still playing with the flower dog?" Bryan, the shorter one, asked one day as I was trying to pull a rope toy out of Maggie Rose's hand. I was very interested in Bryan's arrival because he held some peanut butter pressed between two pieces of bread and was chewing at it. "Perfect dog for you. Look, she's so tiny and weak, she can't even win at tug-of-war!"

Maggie Rose's shoulders hunched stubbornly. "There's nothing wrong with being little," she answered.

Bryan snorted. "Oh, I know. I used to be little, too, when I was a *baby*. Bye, runt." He went on down the hall, taking his peanut butter with him. I watched him leave regretfully.

"There's nothing wrong with being little," my girl repeated softly to me. "Better to be little and nice than big and mean, Lily. Right?"

She let go of the rope toy, so I won! I gripped it in my teeth and shook it hard. Then I ran back to her and plopped the damp bit of rope in her lap so we could play again.

While I tugged, I heard a door open somewhere. Footsteps approached. New people were arriving! I leaped into Maggie Rose's lap so I could check them out from a safe place.

Mom came down the hall, leading another woman, a man, and a boy who was bigger than Maggie Rose but smaller than Bryan. "These are wonderful, active dogs," Mom was saying as they walked. "And they're fine with children. I bring my own kids here to play with the pups regularly to socialize them. They're going to be great family dogs."

Mom and the pack of people she was leading stopped by our kennel. Maggie Rose scooted to one side to give them room. She put both hands around me, and I felt her body tense. Suddenly, she grabbed the front of her T-shirt and pulled its soft folds completely over me.

I was inside my girl's shirt, held against her skin. I wiggled in surprise. Was this a new game? Her heart was pounding. Now Maggie Rose wasn't just unhappy—she was afraid!

I knew there was something I should be doing to help her, because I was her puppy, but what? I could see Maggie Rose's chin up through a small hole at the top of the shirt. Should I try to climb up there?

I heard my brothers yip inside the pen, the wire gate rattling as they jumped up to put their paws against it.

"The spotted one! I want the spotted one!" I heard one of the new boys say.

"Oh," the new woman said. "Is that the mother? I didn't realize these were pit bull puppies. Aren't they . . . dangerous? The breed, I mean."

"No," I heard Mom reply firmly. "There's a lot of misinformation out there. Some of it's ridiculous! Supposedly, pits have special locking jaws, which is of course not true. People also say their brains never stop growing and that the increasing pressure makes them crazy. No idea who would believe *that!* Some pits are trained as attack dogs, which is a shame. But most of them are as gentle as this sweet girl. If you treat them with love and kindness, that's how they will be with people."

"Can I have him?" the boy begged.

"His name is Gunner, but you should feel free to rename him whatever you would like," Mom said.

"Yes," the other lady said. "If that's the one you want, that's the one we'll take."

I felt Maggie Rose relax suddenly. Thank goodness. Whatever was bothering her had stopped being scary. I seized a fold of her T-shirt in my teeth and shook it. Then I wrestled with it.

"Here, Lily," Maggie Rose whispered to me. She picked up the hem of her shirt so I could squirm back out into the light.

That was a strange game. I liked Tug the Rope better.

The new boy had picked up White-Tail-Brother and was holding him under his chin. White-Tail-Brother was wiggling around to lick the boy's neck, just as I liked to do with Maggie Rose.

The new woman and man were smiling as they watched.

"Yes! I want him," the boy insisted, hugging White-Tail-Brother close.

"Okay, then. You've already filled out an application, and we've checked your references, so we're all set!" Mom said.

"We can take him now?" the new woman asked. "We've got a crate in the car."

"Perfect." Mom smiled.

The boy carried White-Tail-Brother away down the hall. He must be going on an adventure. Maybe he was heading Outside! Oscar meowed as they went past, and Freddie the ferret dashed up to his gate to see what was happening and then dived back into his den.

Mom lingered behind to gaze down at Maggie Rose.

"You see, hon? See how happy they were?" she asked gently. "That's how this works. We don't just find new owners; we make families."

My girl didn't answer. She put me back in my pen after a final cuddle and kiss. Her sadness was out in the open again. I sat and stared up at her, wondering if I should have tried to stay under the T-shirt longer.

Later that day, I realized that something very strange had happened. White-Tail-Brother did not come back.

I dodged away from Biggest-Brother, who wanted to sit on me, and nipped at Brown-Brother's nose so that he'd keep his distance. Then I went to my mother, who was sitting up in her corner, watching the gate alertly.

She barked once, sharply. The meaning could not have been more clear—she wanted all of us near her.

I pressed against her side. My brothers stopped splashing in the water bowl and went to her, too.

But White-Tail-Brother did not come. Not ever again. He was gone.

Over the next few days, the same thing happened again. And *again!* New people came and talked and were happy, and when they left, they carried a puppy from my family. Brown-Brother went with a man and three girls who all talked at once. Biggest-Brother was carried away in the arms of a tall young woman wearing jeans and boots and a wide, wide smile.

Maggie Rose was playing with me each time this happened. She kept me in her lap the whole time, which made me feel better when the people left with a brother. Maggie Rose was safety, just like my mother. She had strong arms and a warm lap, and I could feel the love in her hands and hear it in her voice. I knew she would not let anyone take me away.

6

The day after Biggest-Brother left, Maggie Rose came to visit with a new scent on her hands. It smelled like Oscar the cat, except this smell had been left behind by *two* cats! Two different cats, ones I had never met.

"Oh, Lily, the new kittens are so cute!" my girl told me. "I bet you'd like to see them. When they get a little older, you can play together!"

"No way, Maggie Rose," Amelia said from out in the hallway. She was brushing at the floor with a broom.

"Why not?" Maggie Rose asked, looking up from where she was sitting on the floor with me. "They'd have fun."

"It's not worth the risk," Amelia answered. "Somebody could get hurt."

"But Lily wouldn't hurt a kitten," Maggie Rose responded indignantly. "Remember how careful she was with Missy?"

"Maybe she wouldn't mean to. But puppies and kittens play very differently, and it would be easy for one of them to get scared and lash out. Remember when Craig let Freddie out of his cage when a cat was loose? Your mom and I were terrified that one of them would bite the other. We have to keep the animals separate to keep them safe."

"I'll bet that if she got to meet the kittens, Lily would be the gentlest dog in the world," Maggie Rose said.

"Well, you can ask your mother, but I'm willing to bet that she'll say no," Amelia replied.

Amelia swept her way down the hall, and my girl took me to Outside! I looked around to see if I would find my brothers out there, but it was just me and Maggie Rose.

When I squatted in the yard, something marvelous happened—Maggie Rose gave me a treat. "Good dog, Lily! When you go outside, you get a treat."

I loved being good dog, and I loved getting a treat. From that day on, whenever I squatted outdoors, my girl gave me a treat. What a strange and wonderful thing!

And that wasn't all. Maggie Rose also took out a

rope, which she called a *leash*. She came over to me and connected the leash to my collar with a metal buckle. The buckle made a *snick* sound as it latched.

The moment I heard that *snick* sound, Maggie Rose stuck a treat in front of my nose. I gobbled it up. The world was such an amazing place with treats for all these squats and *snicks*!

I soon figured out that a leash was meant to let Maggie Rose drag me in one direction and to let me drag her in another. We played Leash for a while, and then Maggie Rose took the leash off my collar. It made another *snick* sound, but I did not get a treat. Why not?

Maggie Rose found a ball in the grass. She picked it up.

I knew this game! We were going to play Bring It Here!

When we played this game, Maggie Rose would toss a bouncy ball and I would chase it, biting at it and trying to catch it. Once I finally had the thing under control, I would pick it up and drop it back into the grass at my feet.

"Bring it here, Lily!" Maggie Rose would call every time.

I did not know what she was saying, but knew that if I played with the ball long enough, she would come over and try to take it from me, and then I could run away with it. Chase Me!

So that's what I did when Maggie Rose threw the ball. I raced after it and snatched it up and dropped it between my front paws. I looked at Maggie Rose and waited for the chasing.

"Lily," Maggie Rose said to me, "that's not how we play ball! You're supposed to bring it back to me. It's called *retrieving*."

I figured she was telling me that I was doing it correctly because we were both having so much fun. I picked the ball up again and shook my head to show her that I agreed with her.

The back door opened, and Bryan came sauntering out. He stood with his hands in his pockets.

"What'cha doing, runt?" he asked.

"Nothing," Maggie Rose replied in a mumble. She shrugged. "Teaching Lily to retrieve."

"Let's see," Bryan suggested.

"Well, first I have to get the ball from her," my girl explained.

Bryan laughed. I wagged, ready to run! "Okay," he said. And he lurched into motion, thundering straight at me!

Bryan was so much bigger and faster than my girl! And he moved so quickly that he frightened me. I shrank back, cowering on the ground. The ball fell from my mouth. The boy lunged forward and snatched it up. "Got it!" he announced.

"Hey, you scared Lily," Maggie Rose said. "That's not nice."

I glanced at her uncertainly.

"She's a puppy. She'll get over it," Bryan said with a shrug. He wasn't running at me anymore, so I felt better. Also, he still smelled like peanut butter, and it was hard to be frightened of someone who smelled as good as that.

Still, I kept a careful eye on him. I liked Bryan's smells, but I couldn't be sure what he was about to do next. Was he going to run at me again?

"You ready, Lily?"

I heard my name. Bryan had his arm cranked back. I tensed. Then he whipped his hand over his head, and the ball fired straight at the fence. I chased it. But when it hit the wooden barrier, it bounced back so hard it skipped right past me!

I skidded to a stop and spun around, running after it, my mouth open. I snagged that ball on the run, lifting it triumphantly and trotting past my girl and her brother, chewing it proudly.

"Bring it here, Lily!" my girl called. That meant she was going to chase after me very soon and try to grab the ball. Good, I was ready!

"Hey! Bad dog!" Bryan called harshly.

His tone brought me up short. I stared at him, confused. What was his problem?

"No!" Maggie Rose scolded Bryan. "That's not how you do it. Amelia says you train a dog with love and praise and treats, not by yelling at it."

"That's stupid." Bryan snorted. "My soccer coach yells all the time. It's just how you get people to do what you say."

"People, maybe, but not dogs," my girl replied.

I wagged a bit uncertainly. Weren't we going to play ball anymore?

Bryan folded his arms. "Okay, let's see. Try it your way."

"Bring it here, Lily!" Maggie Rose called. There was an odd note in her voice, and I cocked my head at her curiously. I was ready to have her run after me in the yard, playing Bring It Here, but she seemed upset about something.

I let the ball dribble from my mouth and then pounced on it, trying to lure her into chasing me.

"Please, Lily!" Maggie Rose said.

"Stupid dog," Bryan said scornfully.

Maggie Rose whirled on him. "Why do you always have to be mean?"

Bryan blinked. "What?"

"You are always so mean to me!"

I wandered over, ball in my jaws. What had happened to our game?

"I'm mean to you?" Bryan repeated.

"Yes!"

Bryan stared at her. I went to my girl and dropped the ball. It bounced at her feet. Neither one of them seemed to notice.

My girl folded her arms. "Mom says that the kids at school are always picking on you, and that's why you pick on me. And it's not fair."

"They do not," Bryan said. Suddenly, his voice and face were angry. "I can take care of myself at school and everywhere else."

I jumped on the ball, and it skittered away when my front paws hit it. I grabbed it in my mouth. Maggie Rose and Bryan both seemed tense, which was very strange. We had a bouncy ball. What more could they possibly want?

"And I'm not mean," Bryan continued. "Mean is like I hit you or something. I never hit anybody."

"Mean is words, too," Maggie Rose said, looking at him hard.

Bryan put his hands in his pockets and stared at the fence for a moment. I looked in the same direction, but there was nothing to see.

I dropped the ball again. My meaning was clear, but no one seemed to get what they were supposed to do.

People are much more complicated than dogs, I

decided. Or maybe dogs are just smarter, because I had never met one who wouldn't be instantly delighted to have a ball bouncing at their feet.

Bryan looked away from the fence. Maybe he'd figured out that it was not likely to do anything interesting. He scowled at Maggie Rose. "There's nobody in this neighborhood but little kids," Bryan muttered. "Back home, I used to get back from school and play football or basketball with Ricky and Calvin and Jason. Now when I get home from school, there's nothing to do."

"What about soccer?" Maggie Rose asked.

Bryan kicked at the dirt. "I don't have any friends on the team." He sighed. "I'm not very good yet."

"Oh," Maggie Rose replied.

Bryan abruptly left us, going back inside through the door. Maggie Rose crouched and snatched up the ball before I could get it. I was secretly pleased. We couldn't really play Bring It Here unless somebody threw the ball, and I wasn't able to do that myself.

I tensed, crouched, my legs wide, my focus on the ball in her hand. "Get it!" she sang, tossing the ball. It hit the ground with far less force than Bryan had put into his toss, but I was thrilled, anyway. I chased after the toy, grabbing it up.

"Bring it here!" Maggie Rose told me.

I pranced past the fence, the ball in my mouth, ready for her to come after me. I knew she would. And she did! She ran after the ball, and we wrestled for it. I let her tug it out of my mouth after a little bit so that we could start the game all over.

Then the door opened, and Bryan came back out. I halted and regarded him curiously; I had thought he didn't want to play.

Bryan walked up to Maggie Rose. "Here," he said. He thrust something forward.

Treat? I dropped the ball and trotted over to see what we were doing now.

My girl took the object in her hand. When I sat at her feet, I could tell it had almost no odor.

"I got it at the school book fair. See? It's a journal," Bryan said. "All the pages are blank inside. So you can write whatever you want. You can draw pictures or do poems and stuff. A lot of the girls have them in my class."

Maggie Rose was staring at the thing in her hand as if it were a piece of chicken. I wondered if she was going to throw it. Would it bounce like the ball?

"Thank you, Bryan," she whispered.

"So, like, it's personal. Private. That means whatever you write, nobody else can read it except you. Okay? That's the rules for a personal journal."

My girl was smiling. She threw her arms wide and gave Bryan a giant hug.

"Hey," he complained.

"It's the nicest thing you've ever done," Maggie Rose claimed, smiling.

"Yeah, well, whatever," Bryan muttered. He was looking down at the ground and frowning and grinning at the same time. He seemed both tense and really happy, and I could feel the love in him for my girl.

At that moment, I liked Bryan very much, not just because of the peanut butter odor but because he loved Maggie Rose and I did, too.

7

Apparently, we were done with the ball, because we went back inside, leaving the toy forgotten in the yard. It would be there, though, next time we walked through the door!

Bryan went off in another direction, but I stayed with Maggie Rose, who took me down the rows of kennels. Oscar meowed at us, and Maggie Rose stopped to greet him. Then she opened the door to Brewster's pen. Brewster roused himself from his slumber and blinked at us, wagging his tail in a way that I knew meant he didn't want to get out of bed unless a person made him.

"Okay, Lily. Go sit by Brewster. I want to draw a picture of you. I'm going to call it *Lily and Brewster*. Okay?"

I looked at her expectantly. Clearly, something wonderful was about to happen!

Or not. Maggie Rose picked me up and carried me over to Brewster. We sniffed each other. Neither one of us had any idea what Maggie Rose wanted us to do.

"Okay! Good dog! Stay, Lily, stay!"

I looked at Brewster. He looked at me. Sighing, he put his head down. I looked at Maggie Rose.

Now what?

She was bent over the thing that Bryan had handed her out in the yard. She had a stick in her hand and was making faint scratching sounds with it. I yawned.

The thing about Brewster was that his naps were like a leash, pulling me into the same deep sleep. I couldn't keep my eyes open, and soon I was sprawled out next to him. He put his head on my chest, just like my mother dog.

I opened my eyes when Maggie Rose stirred, but Brewster didn't. I wiggled out from under Brewster's head, and he didn't even notice. I bowed and stretched to get rid of the sleepy feeling in my legs, watching my girl for a sign about what we were going to do next.

"Want to see the picture I drew?" my girl asked me. She held out the dry, flat thing that Bryan had handed to her. I sniffed at it politely.

"Want to know what else I did? I wrote a wish, Lily," Maggie Rose said.

I sat and scratched at my ear with my rear paw.

"My wish is about you, Lily. I wrote down that I want you to be my dog forever. I wrote that I hope that every day, when I go to school, you'll come here to be with Mom and Amelia. And when I get home, I'll come straight here to the rescue, and I'll clean the cat cages and fold the towels and do all the work I always do, but you'll be right here with me. And when I go home, you'll go home with me. You'll sleep on my bed. You're my dog, Lily. Mine, and nobody else's."

I wagged because there was something so happy and hopeful in her voice, I could hear it and feel it.

"You know what else, Lily? Bryan isn't so mean after all," Maggie Rose told me.

Several days later, we were back to playing the game with the ball where my girl would throw it, yell, "Bring it back!" and then run after me. I loved that game!

I'd just gotten my teeth on the ball for the tenth time when the back door opened. Maggie Rose looked up. "Hi, Dad!"

"How's my game warden girl today?" Dad replied as he came up to us. He was smiling. I wagged at Dad. We he going to play Bring It Here? Two people chasing me with the ball would be even better than one!

"I'm teaching Lily to retrieve, but she doesn't understand," my girl replied. I wagged at her because she'd said my name.

"Well, I don't want to interrupt your dog training, but I thought you might like to go with me to do something very important," Dad said.

"Can I bring Lily?" Maggie Rose asked eagerly.

Dad nodded. "I knew you'd want to. I already asked your mom, and she said yes."

Just like that, we were done playing. Now, as far as I was concerned, there could hardly be any activity more interesting than a game with a ball. Even so, I eagerly trotted after my girl and Dad as they left the yard. Anything with people is better than anything with just a dog—or even a dog and a ball.

When the leash clicked into my collar, Maggie Rose offered me a treat. Life was great!

This time, she pushed through a different door to go to a new Outside, another yard with a vehicle parked in it. The thing smelled strongly of other places and other things, and I began sniffing it eagerly.

"Hop in the truck, Maggie Rose," Dad said as he opened a back door. My girl climbed into the thing called truck, patting her legs.

"Come, Lily!"

I jumped in, wagging. Maggie Rose unsnicked my

collar—no treat for that. But sometime soon she might reattach it, and I'd get something then!

Dad closed the door, and I watched, excited, as he went around the front of the truck and opened his door and slid in. We had the entire back seat to ourselves!

"When do I get to sit up front with you, Dad?" Maggie Rose asked.

"When you're a little older, honey. Right now, you'd be in danger if the airbag went off."

"When I'm bigger, you mean," Maggie Rose corrected softly. A tinge of sadness mingled in with her words.

"You'll hit a growth spurt soon, I promise. Look at Craig. He's shot up a foot since we moved here."

I jumped down off my girl's lap and settled below her feet. Dad's door shut with a slam, but that didn't bother me. When the floor began to shake and bounce, that didn't bother me, either. I was with my girl and Dad. And coming from the far back of the truck was an animal smell I recognized. Another animal was in here with us! And I was pretty sure I knew who it was!

"Why do you call this a truck, Dad?" Maggie Rose asked. "Craig says it's an SUV."

Dad chuckled. "Right, I guess technically Craig is correct. But to me, it's a truck. Remember that sports car I had back in Michigan? This big old Expedition is as far from a Corvette as you can get, so I call it a truck."

Maggie Rose was quiet for a little while. "Do you miss Michigan?" she asked hesitantly.

"Not at all," Dad replied. "I used to go to an office and stare at a computer screen all day, but now I get to drive up into the mountains and help animals. Your mom's happy, too; after working in that huge hospital for ten years, she gets to do something she's passionate about. The rescue was failing when they put her in charge, and now it's got enough money to keep going, and the volunteers are organized. Why, do you miss where we used to live, Maggie Rose?"

"No, I like helping animals, too."

"That's my game warden girl."

"Bryan wishes we would move back, though."

Dad sighed. "I know. He's still having some trouble adjusting."

"Maybe our family needs a dog," Maggie Rose suggested.

I wagged a little at the word *dog*.

"Oh? Did Bryan say he wants a dog?" Dad asked.

"If he did, could he have one?" my girl countered.

Dad was quiet for a moment. "What are you getting at, Maggie Rose?"

"Lily is the best dog," my girl said in a rush. "She

would help Bryan feel better about living here in Colorado. And me, she would help me feel better, and then I would get straight As and would do all my chores, and I would walk her and clean up after her and feed her. Please, Dad, can I keep Lily?"

"Oh," Dad responded slowly. "Now I get it. Have you already spoken to your mother about this?"

Maggie Rose was silent.

"Honey? What did your mom say?"

"She said maybe not," Maggie Rose mumbled.

"Okay, well, I think we'd better do what your mom says," Dad replied cheerfully. "Right? She's the one who's the expert in animal rescue."

Maggie Rose looked out the window. That sadness was back in her. I sat up and gave her leg a lick to remind her that with a puppy lying under her shoes, there was no reason to be unhappy, but she didn't look down at me, and her mood didn't improve.

For a long time, no one said anything.

"Where are we going today, Dad?" Maggie Rose asked finally.

"Your mom cut the cast off the squirrel this morning, and the squirrel looks fully recovered, so we're letting her loose," Dad answered.

"Sammy? Sammy's a girl?"

I was right! Sammy was the name of the animal I could smell in the back! She was a squirrel!

"Sammy? Is that her name?" Dad replied with a small laugh.

My girl was quiet for a moment. "Samantha," she decided. "*Sammy* is short for *Samantha*."

The motion of the truck vibrated through my body, making me a little sleepy. I yawned.

"Samantha," Dad agreed.

"Are we letting her loose in a park?" Maggie Rose asked.

"Well, no. Samantha's an American red squirrel, and they're territorial. I've been scouting around, and I've found a stand of pine trees near an old storage shed that doesn't have any other squirrels living there."

"So Sammy won't have any friends to play with?" Maggie Rose asked. She sounded a little worried. "Like Bryan?"

"No, but that's okay. *Territorial* means that other squirrels wouldn't want her moving in to their neighborhood, and they'd fight with her. When she's ready to have babies, she'll be very popular with boy squirrels, I promise."

My eyes kept blinking shut. Each time, it seemed harder to open them, so I just gave up. I jerked awake, though, when the truck lurched to a stop.

Maggie Rose clicked a leash into my collar. Treat! She and I slipped out onto some grassy ground, and I shook and then squatted, looking up expectantly at my girl when I was done. Treat!

When I was done with the second treat and realized my girl wasn't going to give me another one, I examined my surroundings. I was amazed. This yard was bigger than any yard I had ever imagined. I smelled clean air, dust, and, farther away, an animal or two I had never met.

The fence, wherever it was, was so far away I couldn't even *see* it! Outside was not only fun, it was *huge!*

If my girl threw the ball here, there was nothing to stop it from bouncing forever. Well, nothing except a good dog who would catch it and then run away from her.

Dad raised the back of the truck and pulled out a cage, and the smell of Sammy instantly filled my nose. A moment later, I saw the squirrel clinging to the wires in the bottom of the cage as Dad shut the back of the truck. My girl and I followed Dad, who walked toward some trees, carrying the cage with him.

When we got to the trees, I could see dry sticks all over the ground. They had an odd, sharp smell. The same smell drifted down from the branches overhead.

Sticks are some of my favorite objects, because any one of them can instantly become a toy, especially if Maggie Rose is holding on to the other end of it. But

these sticks smelled so strongly that I knew they'd leave a real tang on my tongue if I chewed one. I decided to ignore them. It was hard, but I could do it.

"See how the reddish color of the pine needles matches the tint in Sammy's fur?" Dad asked, setting the cage down on the ground. Sammy and I stared at each other, and I wondered if she would be interested in Chase Me. "Good camouflage."

"So they always live in pine trees?" Maggie Rose asked.

"This species does. They mostly eat seeds from pine cones. Have you ever seen a pile of old pine cones under a log or in a hollow by a stone? Red squirrels make those piles to store food for the winter. They're called *middens*."

"Middens," Maggie Rose repeated.

"Squirrels do a lot for the ecosystem. When they gather nuts, they always forget where they put some of them, and nuts are seeds. In the spring, some of them sprout and become new seedlings. A forest with squirrels is a healthy forest," Dad said.

Sammy wasn't moving much, just standing nearly frozen inside the cage. Every so often, she shook her tail a little. That tail looked like it would be a lot more fun than a stick!

I didn't know what we were doing, but it was fun, anyway. Plus, for the moment, Maggie Rose seemed to have forgotten about being sad. I did not believe for a moment that being with a squirrel was what was making her happy. It must be me; I must be doing something right.

Or maybe it was just being out in such a big yard that had cheered Maggie Rose up. It certainly made *me* happy.

Near the trees was an old building with no doors, just walls and a sagging roof. I hoped we were not going to live in *there*. The house had a big yard, but I could not imagine that my mother and my girl and Dad and everyone else could fit along with me into such a small place.

"Do you notice something you don't see?" Dad asked.

"Don't see?" Maggie Rose repeated. She was silent for a moment. "Middens?"

"Exactly!" Dad beamed. "Very good, Maggie Rose. That's one of the ways I figured out that no other squirrels had declared this their territory. No middens."

"I hope Sammy will be happy here," Maggie Rose said.

"Well, there's only one way to find out. Hold on to Lily," Dad advised.

I felt a twist on my collar as Maggie Rose tightened the leash, and I wagged at the sudden attention. Then I tensed as Dad knelt by the cage and began rattling it. Pretty soon, I was going to play with a squirrel!

Sammy retreated from Dad, her fluffy tail twitching. I watched with excitement as the cage door swung open. Yes! Time for Chase Me! I wagged furiously.

Dad stood up and stepped back. "Okay, Samantha," he said.

"Go on, Sammy," Maggie Rose encouraged.

8

Sniffing, Sammy moved with quick, jerky motions toward the front of the cage. I got ready to play, but as I surged forward, my girl held me back.

Bewildered, I glanced up at her. What sort of game was this? We had this enormous yard, but my girl was holding me still? With a squirrel about to be on the loose? Hadn't we been waiting all this time for a chance to play Chase Me with this creature?

Sammy darted out of the open door of the cage and stopped. She was twisting her head back and forth in quick motions, looking. Maggie Rose was tense; I could feel it in the way she held my leash.

What were we doing? I strained against my collar. Squirrel!

"No, Lily," Maggie Rose said.

It was a word I had heard before—*no*—and I didn't like it very much. It meant I was not being a good dog. How could that be? I wasn't doing anything except trying to play with a squirrel!

Suddenly, Sammy skittered forward, halted, and then dashed to a tree, leaping up and scrabbling toward the top branches. I barked in frustration, and Sammy paused on a tree limb, staring down at me.

Well, how was I supposed to play Chase Me when she was up there? I yipped, wagging, and when my girl suddenly dropped my leash, I ran to the tree and put my paws on the trunk and stared up at Sammy. If I looked at her hard enough, she'd understand that she needed to come back down right now!

"Your leg's all better, Sammy!" my girl called, clapping her hands. I wagged. Yes, Sammy, come down to play!

"Maggie Rose, as long as we're here, I'm going to walk out toward the edge of the field. There's a small prairie dog colony out there. I want to see how they're doing. Do you want to come with me or stay with the truck? Lily will have to remain behind; prairie dogs have fleas, and we don't want Lily to get any."

"I'll stay here with Lily and watch Sammy," Maggie Rose replied.

Sammy was still watching from atop the tree. I

decided she wasn't as smart as a dog, because any dog would be able to tell I wanted to play Chase Me. I decided that until the squirrel came to her senses and returned to the ground, I should ignore her. I shook myself all over, brushing away thoughts of Chase Me and ready for whatever came next.

"I won't go far, but if you need me for anything, just honk the horn," Dad said. I wagged as he marched away from us, and I looked up at my girl, who was gazing up into the trees. I followed her gaze but couldn't see anything but a squirrel that I was ignoring.

Maggie Rose undid my leash. "Let's make a midden for Sammy, Lily," Maggie Rose said. She began picking up the dry, pointy balls that were littered on the ground. They had the same sharp tang I could smell coming off the trees. She soon had a pile of them in a hollow area under a fallen tree trunk.

I watched, baffled. What could we possibly be doing now? I was even less interested in these dry things as toys than I was in the sticks with the odor that made my eyes water.

A quick look showed me that Dad had wandered far away. I sat and scratched under my chin with a rear paw, wondering what my humans were doing.

"Sammy! You're on the roof!" Maggie Rose squealed. She ran over to the old building, and I followed. Sammy had made her way there, leaping from branch to branch, and was now on top, peering over the edge at us. "Here, Sammy, have a pine cone!"

My girl swung her arm and tossed one of the odd-smelling balls up in the air and over the squirrel's head. Sammy immediately disappeared from view.

"Squirrels eat pine cone seeds, Lily," Maggie Rose said.

I wagged, then barked when Sammy's head reappeared. Now she was holding the strange ball in her mouth. Suddenly, the ball fell from Sammy's mouth, bounced down the roof, and landed at my feet. I pounced on it, picking it up. But I didn't chew it. It tasted awful.

Maggie Rose laughed delightedly. When she reached to grab the dry, crackly ball out of my mouth, I danced away. We could play Chase Me at last! I was willing to keep this disgusting ball in my mouth if it meant my girl would play at last.

"No, Lily! Bring it here."

Bring it here. That sounded familiar. And there was that word *no* again. I froze. Was Maggie Rose trying to tell me that we were playing Chase Me differently? But how else would the game go? I had the dry, prickly ball in my mouth, and now I would run and Maggie Rose would come after me. Right?

The powerful tang of the ball was building a horrible taste on my tongue. Suddenly, I just needed to spit the thing out.

"Good dog, Lily!" my girl praised.

Good dog? What had I done to get from *no* to *good dog* so quickly? I wagged in confusion.

The squirrel was watching from the roof. Maggie Rose cranked her arm back and pitched the foul-tasting ball up over Sammy's head again.

I was frankly glad to be rid of it.

Sammy vanished. And then she was back with that same awful ball in her mouth! I was immediately worried she would toss it down again. We had enough of them on the ground already; my girl had made a whole pile of the things over by the fallen tree.

"Throw the pine cone!" Maggie Rose encouraged Sammy.

Pine cone. The thing was called a *pine cone,* and it tasted as bad as anything I had ever had in my mouth. I was very disappointed to see Sammy drop it once again. But when it hit the ground, I felt I had to leap on it, because apparently that was the game we were playing.

Maggie Rose laughed with such absolute glee I couldn't help but wag, even with a horrible pine cone in my mouth. My tongue felt sticky.

"Bring it here, Lily!" she sang, holding out her hand.

Apparently, *bring it here* meant I did not have to hold this thing in my mouth any longer. I gladly allowed my girl to take it from my jaws.

"We're playing catch! Catch, Sammy!"

The game lasted for some time, until my tongue and nose were so full of that piney flavor I felt pretty sure I would never be able to taste food again. I would have been more than happy to do anything else, but my girl was laughing so delightedly I stuck with it. Wasn't this what I wanted, to hear her clear, high laughter? I had managed to bring real cheer to my girl, and that was the purpose of a puppy.

Although I did think we could have managed without the pine cone. And probably without the squirrel, too.

Dad came back from wherever he'd been, his dusty boots coated with a new and interesting odor. He poured some water into a bowl for me, and I drank and drank, tasting pine cone with every swallow. Then he put Sammy's cage in the truck, but Sammy forgot to climb in it.

"We played catch with Sammy, Dad!" Maggie Rose said once we were back in the truck. I sprawled at her feet. Exhausted, I yawned so hugely the muscles in my jaw ached. I hoped as soon as Sammy came out of the tree and got in the truck we would go home so I could nap with my mother and maybe my girl and Dad.

"That's nice, Maggie Rose," Dad replied.

"No, really!"

The truck rumbled to life and started moving. Sammy was being left behind. How odd. I decided that I would think about what that meant some other time.

"I have to stop by the house for something," Dad said as we drove. "Then we'll head back to the shelter and drop Lily off."

It was the last thing I heard anyone say before I dozed off.

When the car stopped, I jumped out with Maggie Rose, who put the leash on me. Treat! I looked around to see where we were.

We had not returned to the place where I lived with my mother. We were in a small yard in front of a building that was bigger than the one where Sammy had sat on the roof. The grass and the dirt and the sidewalk all smelled powerfully of Maggie Rose and her family. Dad, Mom, Bryan, Craig, and my girl had walked here many, many times.

That meant this place was all right by me.

Craig was Outside, playing with a big ball. As I watched, he threw it up at the roof, even though there were no squirrels up there. Instead, there was a ring of metal. The ball bounced off the ring and came back down.

Maybe that's how people played Bring It Here when they didn't have any squirrels or pine cones.

"Hey, where you been, runt?" Craig asked.

Dad came around the front of the truck. "Craig? What did you just say?" he demanded.

9

I glanced up at Craig because he was suddenly different. Not afraid, just uncomfortable and tense.

"Uh . . . ," Craig said.

"You called Maggie Rose a runt. Runt? Explain yourself," Dad said.

"It's just a nickname we call her sometimes. Bryan does it, too."

"Don't hide behind your little brother," Dad said shortly.

"It's okay, Daddy. I don't mind," Maggie Rose said quickly.

"No, honey, it's not okay. Craig, your brother is younger, and I don't expect him to behave in a mature fashion, but you're different. You're in high school now. You should be watching out for your sister, not putting her down. Understand?"

Craig kicked the dirt. "Yeah."

"Sorry?" Dad responded.

Craig straightened. "Yes. Sorry."

"All right, then. Maggie Rose, thank you for helping me today with Samantha."

"You're welcome, Dad."

Dad left.

"Craig, I'm sorry. I didn't mean to get you in trouble," Maggie Rose told her brother. "I don't mind it that much. I really am a runt, just like Lily. That's why we belong together."

I wagged at my girl for saying my name.

"No, Dad's right," Craig answered. "Forget it. I won't call you *runt* anymore."

"Dad sometimes calls me *princess*. You can call me that if you'd like." Maggie Rose sounded relieved.

Craig shook his head. "Pass."

"How about smartest kid in the family?" Maggie Rose suggested.

Both Craig and my girl laughed, so I wagged again. "You're the smartest *girl* in the family, though," Craig agreed.

"You should have seen what happened with Samantha, Craig! She played catch with Lily and me."

"Samantha?" Craig replied.

"The squirrel with the hurt leg? Dad took us to her new territory."

"Uh-huh," Craig said slowly. "Catch with a squirrel."

"Really! I'm not lying."

"So maybe that's your new nickname. Squirrel Girl," Craig observed.

Maggie Rose shook her head. "You don't believe me."

Craig shrugged. "I believe you *think* you played catch with a squirrel named Samantha. And wait, what did you mean about Lily? You said you belong together?"

Maggie Rose sighed. "I asked Dad if I could keep her. To be my dog."

Craig lifted his eyebrows. "Wow. What did he say?"

"He didn't say no," my girl replied carefully.

"So he said to ask Mom, right? I bet I know what her answer was. You probably don't remember, but I wanted a Labrador puppy last Christmas, but Mom said she doesn't support giving puppies as gifts because too often they wind up being neglected." Craig shook his head. "She said it would send the wrong message. She didn't say who would get the message, just that it was the wrong one."

"We would never neglect a dog!" Maggie Rose declared hotly.

"I know! I guess Mom's worried about what people

will think. All those volunteers at the shelter. She feels like she needs to set an example."

"Well . . . maybe it will be different with Lily," my girl said hopefully.

Craig smiled. "That would be okay by me," he said. He put his hand down, and I sniffed it, smelling dirt and sweat and something sweet. No peanut butter, though.

Then I squatted.

Treat!

Dad came back out of the house, and Maggie Rose and I rode in the truck to the shelter. I was glad to get to my mother, to snuggle into her warm fur and take a good long nap after all the excitement.

The next day, Maggie Rose came back—of course, because she was my girl! We went out into the yard to play Bring It Here. What a great game!

"Bring it here, Lily," Maggie Rose kept saying.

I ran away from her and pretended that the ball had slipped out of my jaws. When she took a step toward me, I snatched it up again and pranced away so that she'd have to chase me some more.

But then Maggie Rose did something strange. She stopped running after me and instead stood still with her hand out. "Bring it here!"

On purpose, I let the ball go. It rolled a little bit away from me. I glanced at Maggie Rose slyly, thinking she would be unable to resist. As soon as she made her move, I would pounce on the ball and be off.

But Maggie Rose just stood there.

"Bring it here," she repeated.

Why didn't she come get the ball and throw it again? I bowed down, the toy between my forelegs, waiting. But she didn't move.

When we had been playing with the squirrel, *bring it here* meant give the wretched-tasting ball to Maggie Rose so she could pitch it up over Sammy's head. But there was no squirrel here, and this ball was bouncy and it didn't taste awful on my tongue, so . . .

She still held out her hand.

So . . .

Did *bring it here* mean that I should take Maggie Rose the ball? Did that make any sense at all? I danced with the ball, twisting, losing it out of my mouth, jumping on it, wagging, playing, and still Maggie Rose stood with her hand out. "Bring it here," she insisted.

I moved closer, dropping the ball and batting at it, and it rolled right up to her feet.

"Good dog, Lily!"

When my girl bent over to pick the ball up, I tensed, ready to run. There was no time to wag because she was tossing the ball and it was bouncing! I jumped on it triumphantly.

"Bring it here," Maggie Rose called as I ran around the yard with it.

It didn't seem right, but if this was how she wanted to do it, I was not going to fight it. We played and played with the bouncy ball, and I brought the ball to Maggie Rose's feet every time.

After a while, I could see that Maggie Rose was getting a little tired of throwing the ball. I could have kept at it all until dark, but Maggie Rose seemed to feel differently. She led me back into the building. Just inside the door was a bowl of water, and I eagerly lapped some up while Maggie Rose stood by.

People are funny. They never drink out of bowls on the floor, even though there is always one somewhere with some water in it. Instead, they prefer to drink out of much smaller bowls that they hold in their hands.

Mom and Dad were talking down the hall. I felt Maggie Rose tense a little bit as she listened.

"We have that family coming in today who were so interested in adopting Lily. They are really looking forward to meeting her." That was Mom talking. Her voice settled differently on my ears than my girl's—lower and with softer edges.

"How does Maggie Rose feel about that?" Dad asked. His voice caused a rumble in my ears like the sound Oscar made sometimes.

Mom sighed. "Honestly, I didn't even tell her. I think

it would be better to wait until we have a final answer on this family and then explain to her that as much as we all love Lily, we can't possibly keep her. We're so busy right now. Plus I can hardly, as the president of this rescue, have a foster failure in my own family, especially with such an adoptable puppy. It makes me look like a hypocrite."

"It's your decision," Dad replied. "You have to do what's right for the rescue."

"That's an interesting response, James. So you disagree? You think we should keep Lily?"

Maggie Rose drew in a sharp breath. I looked up at her in surprise.

"No, I meant that it's your decision," Dad replied. "It'll break Maggie Rose's heart at first, but she's young, and eventually, she'll forget all about the dog."

"So I get to be the bad guy here?" Mom asked.

"That's not what I said," Dad protested. "What I am saying is that I want to support *you*."

There didn't seem to be any problem that I could see—just people talking, the way they like to do. I went back to getting a good long drink.

"The rescue is running far better, but you still feel new to the job," Dad went on. "If you think adopting one of your own puppies would be a problem, I believe you. But I also get how difficult it will be for Maggie Rose. If you want me to tell her it's our decision, I will."

There was a long silence. "No," Mom said, "I should be the one who tells her. But I really appreciate that you would do it."

Maggie Rose made a tiny sound. I stopped drinking and stared up at her. She seemed so tense, so sad, I felt sure there was something going on, but I did not understand what. Was she sad that we were not playing with the bouncy ball anymore? Was I being a bad dog? I put my paw on her leg and stared up into her face.

"They're coming for you *today*, Lily," she whispered. "I can't let that happen!"

A good puppy would make her girl feel happy. But right now it did not seem that I could do it. Maggie Rose did not even kneel down to cuddle me. She just let her head droop and stared at the floor.

"I'll tell you what," Dad said. "We had such a good time together yesterday releasing the squirrel back into the wild. I'll take Maggie Rose with me this afternoon. We'll ride up into the mountains, and it will keep her mind off Lily. The new people can come meet her, and if everything is successful, we can explain to Maggie Rose that there is another family who loves Lily just as much as she does."

"That is not true," Maggie Rose whispered to me. "Nobody loves you as much as I do, Lily. Nobody."

"That's a really good idea," Mom agreed. "If everything looks good, I'll let them take Lily home with them today on a trial basis. When you and Maggie Rose get back, it will already be settled."

Not long afterward, I heard Dad coming down the hall toward us. He reached down and held out his hands to me, and I sniffed them but stayed with Maggie Rose. She was my girl.

"Hey, Maggie Rose," Dad said. "How would you like to ride with me to do some work? I have to go survey a mountain goat herd up above Echo Lake."

"What's *survey* mean?" Maggie Rose asked.

"I just need to check on the population of mountain goats and see how many there are. Does that sound like fun?"

Maggie Rose swept me into her lap and held me tightly. "Can Lily come?"

Dad chuckled. "Well, no, that's not a good idea."

Maggie Rose looked up at him stubbornly. "Why not?"

"Let's just have it be you and me, okay?" Dad replied. "I think Lily should stay here at the rescue. Why don't you put this puppy back in her kennel and head on out to the truck. I'll be joining you out there in just a minute."

Dad walked out, leaving us by ourselves. "Come with me," Maggie Rose whispered in my ear. "But don't make any noise, okay?"

I did not know what we were doing, but I was happy

to be carried by my girl. She stopped and opened the door to a very tiny room that had no space for anything except shelves and things stacked on the floor. A wave of new odors greeted me. I wagged, eager to explore everything I could smell, but my girl did not set me down. Instead, she reached in and pulled out a small bag and set it on the floor. With a quick zipping sound, she opened it. She threw the top flap back, and I stared curiously into what smelled like a cat bed.

"Okay, Lily," my girl whispered, "I know you are not going to understand any of this, but I need you to get into this carrier and be really, really quiet."

I understood something was being asked of me and wondered if maybe we were about to play Bring It Here with the bouncy ball again.

Maggie Rose leaned over and dropped me gently into the bag. I was delighted at all the animal smells—it was a cat bed! I had my nose to the soft padding when there was a sudden movement and the flap came down over my head. There came a zipping noise. I realized I was now inside the cat bed!

10

Maggie Rose picked up the entire bed with me in it. I spread out my paws as the thing swung back and forth, trying to keep my balance.

Nothing like this had ever happened to me before.

We moved quickly and quietly down the hallway and out a door, and soon we were at Dad's truck. Maggie Rose opened the back door and put my cat bed on the floor between the seats. I stared up through the mesh top at her, utterly bewildered.

"Okay, Lily," she said urgently. "Please be quiet. Okay? Please be quiet. Be quiet."

Obviously, *be quiet* meant to do something, but I had no idea what. Bark?

Maggie Rose shut the door. Her feet dangled above

me. The mesh top of the cat bed was sort of like a blanket; it was soft, and when I pushed my nose against it, I could make it move. But I could not climb past it to get to my girl. I wagged, pretty confused by all of this.

"Okay, Lily," my girl said, "just one more thing. I promise you, this is all going to be fine, but I need you to be really, really quiet. Okay? Be quiet."

There were those words again. Maybe they had something to do with what happened next, which was that a blanket came down and landed on top of the cat bed.

Now I could not see my girl! What were we doing?

The blanket smelled like a lot of dogs. I liked that part but wanted to be able to see Maggie Rose.

I heard another door open and shut and immediately smelled Dad.

"Fasten your seat belt, honey," Dad said.

I felt the truck start to move with a lurch.

This was all very strange. I did not understand why I was lying in a cat bed with a blanket over it. Last time I was in the truck, I was allowed to sit at my girl's feet. This was not the same thing at all!

Probably Maggie Rose would figure that out soon. Any moment, she would whip off the blanket and let me out. Dad would be so happy to see me!

But Maggie Rose didn't seem to get it. I tried to be patient, but after what seemed like a long, long time, I begin to worry that my girl had forgotten all about me.

We were bouncing along, and no one was paying me any attention.

I was her dog! How could she possibly forget me?

Unable to take it any longer, I finally let out a small whine. Not a loud one, just a tiny cry to remind her I was still stuck inside this cat bed.

There was no response at all. Well, if there is anything a puppy knows how to do, it's to make noise. I squealed a little louder.

"What in the world was that?" Dad exclaimed.

"What was what?" Maggie Rose responded.

No one had said my name yet. No one seemed to be planning to let me out of this cat bed. I tried an even louder whine.

"That!" Dad said. "There's an animal in here!"

"An animal?" Maggie Rose replied innocently.

"Maggie Rose," Dad said, "don't play games with me. Is there something you want to tell me?"

"Want to tell you?" Maggie Rose repeated. "No, Daddy, there is nothing that I *want* to tell you."

"All right," Dad said. "Is there something that you *need* to tell me?"

"That you are a very good driver?"

Well, time for me to get serious. I barked.

"Maggie Rose," Dad asked pleasantly, "what just barked from back there?"

"A puppy?" Maggie Rose guessed.

"Did you hide a dog in the back with you?" Dad asked.

"Yes, but, Dad, there were some people coming to take Lily away!" Maggie Rose replied in a rush. "She wouldn't understand! She knows I'm her person! She'd think I was giving her up!"

Just then there was an odd tinkling sound from up near Dad. "That's your mom calling," I heard him say. "My guess is that she figured out that Lily isn't in her pen. Hang on." The truck swerved, got slower, and stopped. "Hello? Hi, honey. I think I might know why you're calling."

Dad was quiet for a moment, but I heard my girl twisting in her seat.

"Right. I guess Lily is in a pet carrier in the back. Maggie Rose was just explaining why disobeying her parents was a good idea."

Dad was quiet, the girl was quiet, I was quiet. "I will have that conversation with her, yes," Dad said. "Talk to you soon, Chelsea. Love you, too."

Dad was silent for a time. I prepared myself to bark again. "That was your mother, Maggie Rose."

"Uh-huh," my girl said.

"Maggie Rose, you have to know that taking Lily without permission was wrong. Your mother was worried when she found that she'd lost a puppy from the shelter."

"But, Dad, they wanted to take Lily away from me!" Maggie Rose cried.

My girl needed me! I barked again. The blanket came off, and I could see Dad peering at me between the front seats. I wagged at him frantically. Maggie Rose hadn't figured out that it was past time to let me out of here, but Dad would surely know!

I was right! Dad reached down, and there was the same strange sensation of moving and tilting as he picked up the cat bed. He opened it, and I surged out, licking his face. He chuckled. Then he put the cat bed down, placing it at my girl's feet. I stood up on my back legs and licked her feet and knees. I was so happy to see her!

"Okay. Good dog. Lie down, Lily." My girl pushed me firmly, and I understood she wanted me to stop trying to climb up. I sat in the open cat bed and gazed up at her adoringly.

Soon we were moving again. "Maggie Rose," Dad said after a long moment of no talking, "your mom runs an animal rescue. And the job of rescue is to find homes for creatures who are lost or abandoned."

"Lily could live at *our* home," Maggie Rose replied instantly. I wagged at the sound of my girl saying my name.

"We will get a dog someday, Maggie Rose, but right now we just have too much going on with your brothers'

sports, your school, and our work. It will be much better when you're older and can take care of a puppy."

"I can take care of Lily *now*," she said insistently. "I promise!"

Dad sighed. "It's a lot more complicated than that. Your mother is the boss of the rescue, but she reports to the board members. Do you know what that means? The board of a rescue are the people who make the important decisions. So your mom is the boss, but the people on the board are *her* bosses. Your mother always has to keep that in mind. Also, your mother must consider what the volunteers who work there would think, not to mention the people who donate money to the shelter. How is it going to look if your mother breaks her own rules and keeps the best puppy for herself?"

I could clearly see and smell my girl's feet, which was nice. I was much happier than I had been when I was underneath a blanket. I stretched out for a nap because it was, after all, a bed—a cat bed, but still a bed.

"Dad, *please*. I promise I will take care of Lily," Maggie Rose begged. "I promise I will feed her and walk her and clean up her messes in the yard, and I'll give her baths and play with her every day. *Please*."

"Hang on, honey," Dad said. "I'm getting another call."

My girl made a frustrated noise. The truck stopped

once more, and Maggie Rose leaned forward and put her hand down inside my cat bed. I sniffed her fingers and then gave her a lick. I wanted her to know that even though we were having a very strange day and I was sitting in a small bag at her feet, I loved her and she would always be my girl. Nothing could ever change that.

"All right, I should be there in about ten minutes. Bye," Dad said. The truck began to move once more. "Maggie Rose, we're going to have to check out the mountain goats some other day. That was a call from the sheriff's department; they've got a deer caught up in a wire fence. I guess it's in a pretty bad way."

"Oh no! Can you help it?" Maggie Rose cried.

I looked up at her with concern. She sounded very alarmed about something and needed her puppy in her lap. I sat up, preparing for the leap.

"I hope I can help it. We'll just have to see," Dad replied. "Sometimes the deer cut themselves on the wire, trying to get free, but usually the wounds are very shallow. The biggest danger comes from their reaction when people approach. That's when deer get frantic and can really hurt themselves."

"I'll help," Maggie Rose proclaimed.

Dad chuckled. "That's my game warden girl, but no, you're not going to help. If a trapped deer is kicking and struggling, it can injure people. These are always tricky situations. We'll have to see when we get there if we can help it or not. Sometimes we can't."

"Then what?" my girl wanted to know.

Dad was silent for a moment. "It's the worst part of my job," he finally replied, "but we can't allow animals to suffer needless pain. If it comes to that, Maggie Rose, I'll tell you so that you can look away."

I felt a flash of worry and anxiety from my girl. Now! I leaped and made it into her lap! "Lily!" my girl said with a surprised laugh, her mood instantly better. "No, you silly dog, you have to get down."

I was amazed and baffled when she dumped me back into the cat bed. I had just been doing my most important job, and it was much easier to do it on her lap than at her feet!

When the truck stopped, Dad got out, and Maggie Rose bent down to pick me up. Finally! I licked and licked my girl while she giggled and turned her face from side to side so I could kiss every bit of her. "Enough! Stop, Lily!" she laughed. I heard my name and figured she wanted me to keep kissing.

Dad left the truck, shutting his door behind him, but after a long moment he came back and opened a door behind us. I turned to try to climb up Maggie Rose and over the seat to see him, but my girl held me tightly. "Well, I'm afraid it's bad," he said.

"Oh no," Maggie Rose said softly.

I heard Dad opening some bags and moving things around. "She's really bound up. We can't just cut the wires; we need to untangle her. Right now, her back is to us, and her nose isn't good enough to know we're there, but the second she catches sight of people, she's going to start kicking." He shut the back door and opened the one next to us. "The good news is that she's not injured; she's up against the fence post on one side, and it's keeping her from fighting the wire. Maggie Rose, I want to try something. It's a crazy idea, but it just might work. Do you think I could borrow Lily for a little bit?"

11

I heard the question in Dad's voice when he said my name, and I wagged a little.

"Sure, Dad. You can take Lily," my girl replied.

I was happy that they were both talking about me.

Dad reached for me. His hands were so much larger than Maggie Rose's that they felt as if they were wrapping my entire body in fingers. I heard the *snick* of my leash clicking into place on my collar and turned quickly to my girl, who understood and held out a treat that I gobbled up instantly.

Then I got ready for a walk, but Dad lifted me up and carried me. He shut the door, and I stared in concern; my girl was still in the truck! She waved and smiled at me through the window, which I recognized as meaning she was happy, but how could she be happy if the two of us were separated?

Dad carried me over to where two people were standing and smiling. As he did, a powerful, wild animal scent reached me, sharp on the air. I glanced around, trying to see what it was.

"So here's my idea," Dad said, still holding me.

I wagged at the two people, my nose still full of the smell of the new animal. It smelled big. It smelled tired and frightened and hurt.

One of the people Dad was talking to was a woman with long hair, and one was a man with short hair. They both wore dark clothes and were happy to see me because I am a puppy. I had the sense that the strange animal scent was coming from somewhere just behind them, but Dad's big hands still gripped me too tightly to allow me to wriggle for a better view.

"Where the deer is bound up in the wire, she can't see down into the drainage ditch right in front of it. There's a mound of earth that blocks the view," Dad continued. "So I'm thinking if one of you went into the ditch—you won't even need to crouch over much—and put this puppy, still on her leash, up where the deer can see her, I can sneak up behind while she's distracted and inject her with ketamine. She'll go right to sleep and we can cut her loose from the wires."

"Wait, won't she panic when she sees a dog?" the

woman asked. I could smell that she had recently been petting a cat. It was too bad that she had to settle for that instead of a dog. I had cat friends back home, but nothing is better than a puppy.

"In my experience, most animals don't find a puppy to be very threatening. I think the deer will be curious more than anything. And if I know Lily, she'll be acting full-on happy dog, which should be both nonaggressive and pretty distracting. I've never tried anything like this before, but I've seen sheep stare at an active puppy like they're hypnotized." Dad shrugged. "The worst thing that could happen is the deer is afraid and starts to kick, but anything else we do is going to cause the same reaction."

"Might work," the man agreed. He had not been near any cats as far as my nose could tell. "If we get into the ditch out of the doe's eyesight, the first thing she'll be aware of is when the puppy pops up." He chuckled. "That'll take her mind off the fence for sure."

"I'll take this sweet little girl into the ditch, if you'd like," the woman offered. "I'm shorter, so there's less a chance the deer will see me."

"Thanks, Officer Simmons," Dad replied. "Her name is Lily." I wagged at Dad.

The woman reached out and took me from Dad, the leash trailing below me into the grass. Besides cat on her hands, I could also smell peanut butter, which made me think of Bryan's breath. "Hi, Lily," she said softly. "Want to see a deer?"

The woman did the strangest thing! At first, she gripped me as securely as Dad had done, carrying me against her chest, and I found myself wishing that Maggie Rose would come out of the truck and show these people the right way to walk with a dog. Finally, she put me down, and I squatted (but the woman didn't even know enough to give me a treat for doing this, even though I was in Outside).

Then we climbed down a short hill, winding up in a narrow place with walls made of earth on either side. Now I could no longer see Dad and the other man, though I could smell both of them still up there somewhere. The woman was walking oddly, bent over at the waist. I trotted happily along the dirt at her feet. We were moving toward that strange new animal smell!

Then for the most bizarre part of all, the woman picked me up and slowly lifted me along the steep slope of one dirt wall. Just short of the top, she let me go. She still kept hold of my leash, though, so I wasn't free to run.

This was simply bewildering, but I was more than willing to go along with whatever we were doing. The woman was still hunched down, gripping my leash, and for a moment I considered leaping back into her arms, but then I decided to climb up toward Dad's scent. As soon as I cleared the lip of the small hill, however, I stopped dead.

Staring at me was a giant creature with black eyes and a white chest. She was lying in some wires, her forelegs crossed in front of her. One of her ears twitched. My nose told me that *this* was the source of the smell I'd noticed before!

Well, I certainly wanted to get to know this new not-dog! Unfortunately, the moment I started to run to her, the leash pulled me up short. This was frustrating; I wanted to play! I bowed, wagging, so that my big, strange new friend would come wrestle.

The animal didn't move at all. I saw Dad moving slowly toward her from behind, some unknown toy in his hand. I yipped, spun in a circle, and then sat, wagging, waiting for the big creature to do something besides just lie there, but she simply stared. Probably she had never seen anything so wonderful as a puppy before and didn't know how to behave.

I hoped that whatever Dad had in his fist was the kind of toy that bounced. When he threw it, I would run after it, and so would this big not-dog. If the big animal didn't already know how to do Bring It Here, I would show her.

That was such an exciting thought that I had to bound up and spin around again, and the not-dog was still staring at me when Dad's arm came down right on

its flank. The creature started jerking and kicking wildly, the wires making loud noises as she thrashed. Dad jumped away. I stopped moving and watched, concerned. I could tell that the animal was in pain and fear.

And then, just like that, the big creature decided to take a nap. Her head drooped, her legs went slack, and her bright black eyes stared at the ground.

"Okay, Officer Simmons," Dad called. "It worked. You can come on up!"

Behind me, the woman stood upright, and then, grunting a little, she scrambled up the slope next to me. "Good dog!" she praised me. "You're so sweet. Can I take you home?"

"She *is* up for adoption," Dad replied.

I wanted to go sniff the exotic odors clinging to the limp animal in the fence, but the woman kept her tight hold on my leash.

"Really? You're looking for a home for Lily?" the woman asked. I wagged at my name.

"Dad? Can I come out now?" my girl called from her open window.

"It's safe, honey," Dad told her.

I wagged. My girl was coming, my girl was coming! When Maggie Rose arrived to talk to us, bending down toward me, I leaped up, straining against the rope holding me, licking her face.

"Lily! You silly, I was right there the whole time!" Maggie Rose sputtered at me.

"Silly Lily!" the woman exclaimed with a grin. "Is that her nickname?"

"Sure!" my girl replied, smiling back.

"That deer was so amazed to see a puppy, your dad was able to sneak right up and inject her," the man next to Dad said to my girl.

"Good dog, Silly Lily!" Maggie Rose exclaimed.

I loved *good dog*. Next to *treat*, it was becoming my favorite word.

"The drug works fast. She conked out before she was able to do any damage to herself," Dad said.

I sat with my girl in the grass while Dad and the other two grown people petted the napping animal and yanked at the fence. When one of the wires snapped back, curling up, I jumped in surprise.

"It's okay, Lily," my girl told me, rubbing my chest. I loved that and felt myself getting sleepy, there in the sunshine. I wondered if Maggie Rose and I would be allowed to go over and nap with the snoozing animal.

"That does it," Dad said to the people helping him pet the animal. "You two might as well take off. We'll hang around for a while, until she shows signs of waking up, so that we can keep her safe from predators and make sure she's okay."

The man turned away, but the woman came to see

me, picking me up. "Oh, Silly, Silly Lily, I don't think I have ever seen a puppy so cute as you. Would you like to come live with me?"

She was holding me right up to her face, so I felt I had no choice but to lick her nose. She laughed and set me down next to Maggie Rose, who had grown suddenly sad for some reason. I climbed into my girl's lap, licking and wagging, using all of my puppy love to make her happy again.

The two others left, but Dad and Maggie Rose stayed with me. "How would you feel if Lily went to live with Officer Simmons?" Dad asked. "Would you like that, Maggie Rose?"

Maggie Rose lifted me to her lips and kissed the top of my head.

"Honey?"

"I want to keep Lily," Maggie Rose insisted softly.

Dad sighed. "Oh, Maggie Rose," he said.

12

For a long, long time, nobody moved or said anything. The sheer pleasure of being in my girl's lap lulled me into a deep nap, but I became instantly alert when Dad stood. "Looks like the deer's starting to wake up."

The big animal had been sleeping motionless on the ground, but now her thin legs were twitching. Maggie Rose jumped to her feet, so I did too, yawning. Nap time was over for all of us. I was ready to play with my new friend!

"Okay, let's get back to the truck. We don't want to frighten her," Dad said.

I was disappointed when we left the huge not-dog and returned to the truck. I sat in my girl's lap and alertly watched out the window because that's what Maggie Rose and Dad were both doing. I didn't see any squirrels or anything else that could be keeping their attention, though. Just the same animal who was taking a nap the way old Brewster did.

Naps were just about *all* that Brewster did.

At last, the big animal staggered to her feet. *Now* she wanted to play? But we were all in the truck! I wagged, waiting for Maggie Rose to open the door and let me out. I watched as the creature took a few steps. Her back legs seemed to fold up, and she almost fell. Then she staggered up to all four feet again. She took a few more steps. Then with a flash, she was running away, not galloping but jumping up and down as she bolted. I yipped with excitement.

"There she goes!" Maggie Rose sang.

"That's a sight I never get tired of seeing," Dad replied with a huge smile. "An animal set free to return to where it belongs."

"But not dogs," Maggie Rose pointed out.

"Oh no. There is no such thing as a free dog, just abandoned ones. We humans took over canine breeding a long time ago. We bred them to be dependent on us. Dogs are really only happy when they're with people."

My girl stroked me, and I shivered with pleasure.

Dad started the truck. "Let's go back to the rescue," he said. "Maggie Rose, you know you're going to have to talk to your mother about what you did."

My girl kicked her legs. "I know," she replied quietly.

When we arrived back home, Mom sat with my girl at a table while I sprawled, exhausted, at their feet. What a day!

"This is serious, Maggie Rose," Mom said in grave tones. "You took Lily without permission. Do you want me to make a rule that you can no longer come here to the rescue?"

"*No!*" my girl blurted, her voice so full of fear and emotion that I climbed to my feet and went over and sat beside her, staring up at her in concern.

"Then you must promise to never do anything like that again," Mom continued. "I appreciate when you help us here, I really do, but you cannot interfere with our operations. Do I have your word?"

"But . . . but . . . ," My girl protested weakly.

"What is it?" Mom asked.

"But Lily helped save a deer! It was caught in a fence and would have hurt itself and might have had to be put down, but it didn't see Dad with his shot because Lily was jumping around. If I hadn't taken Lily with us, something bad could have happened."

I nosed my girl's leg to let her know I knew she was talking about me.

"I understand what you're saying, Maggie Rose," Mom replied. "It was a happy accident. But you didn't take Lily with you to help; you took her for an entirely different reason. And you know I would have said no if you had asked, because there was a family coming to see her. They left to go to a different shelter, and they called to say that they found a puppy that they're happy with, but they might have been just as happy with Lily."

"Then Lily saved *two* animals," Maggie Rose responded. "The deer and a puppy at another shelter!"

Mom shook her head. "We owe it to Lily to find her a good home," she said firmly.

"She has a good home! With me!" Maggie Rose insisted.

Mom pursed her lips. "We're not going to talk about this further," she replied. "We have to go home. Say good-bye to Lily."

My girl hugged me and kissed me, and I tried to lick away her sadness as she carried me back to my pen. She set me gently inside, and then her smell and Mom's drifted away.

It was just my mother and me all alone in our kennel. I had always thought I had too many brothers, but lately I was thinking that it was actually worse to have no brothers at all. My mother did not want to play, and my girl was gone. I was bored and missed my littermates. Most of all, I missed Maggie Rose.

So when a new man came to the gate, I was happy to run to greet him.

Amelia was with him, and she opened up the gate so that I could jump out to see both of them. "Here's the last puppy left from this litter," she said. "Her name is Lily."

My mother hung back, but I was excited to make a new friend. I wriggled at his feet, sniffing his shoes. Shoes were always so fascinating to me because they carried so many scents with them.

Big hands came down and scooped me up, and the man held me so that I could see his face. He wore a soft shirt that smelled a little like Freddie the ferret, and he also wore fur on his face like a cat. I'd never seen a human with fur on his face! I wiggled in close to sniff it and lick it. It smelled of something sweet and soapy, and also of ham and coffee and sugar. Face fur was wonderful!

"She's tiny, but she's not shy, is she?" the man said, laughing.

"One of our volunteers has worked very hard on socializing her," Amelia said, and there was something just a little bit sad in her voice. I cocked my ear at her. Why was *she* sad? Weren't we all making friends?

I was beginning to worry that I wasn't very good at

121

being a puppy. Otherwise, why couldn't I cheer anybody up?

"She's perfect! Can I have her?" the man asked. *He* seemed happy, anyway.

"Well, we ask that everyone use the application process," Amelia said. "And there's an interview with our director, and we check references. But yes, if you want Lily, I'm sure that can be arranged."

The man held me out a little from his face so that he could examine me all over.

"You're going to be my dog!" he told me. "Would you like that? Want to come home with me?"

I wondered what he was talking about. And when was Maggie Rose going to come back? She'd probably like to meet this man with the furry face. We could all be friends together.

The man put me down and picked up a scrap of cloth. He dragged it along the floor, and I jumped on it, seizing it in my jaws and growling as I set my paws and he pulled me back and forth, laughing. He tickled my tummy and kissed my nose. I wagged at the strong gusts of affection coming off him and was disappointed when he finally put me back with my mother and departed, following Amelia.

The day after I'd met my new friend, my girl returned. I was so happy to greet her! I licked her face, trying to tell her how I'd met a new friend and it had been fun playing with him, but of course nobody was like my girl.

Maggie Rose picked me up and tucked me under her arm and then carried me into the hallway. I squirmed a little. I didn't really mind her carrying me, but it was more fun to be on the floor with her. We couldn't play a lot of games when I was in her arms.

I could feel that Maggie Rose was nervous. I licked her shoulder so she'd know I was there to take care of her.

"Come on, Lily," she whispered. "Mom and Amelia are having a meeting, and nobody else is working in the shelter right now. We're going to try something new. I'll prove to them that you're meant to be a rescue dog. Then they won't let anybody else adopt you."

She sounded very determined. I wondered what on earth she was talking about and if it involved food at all.

Maggie Rose took me past Brewster's pen. Our eyes met, but he didn't get up from his nap. We passed another pen that still smelled like Poppy, the black, shaggy dog who had stayed with us for a little while. Then we moved on to the part of the room that had cages stacked on top of one another. Freddie the ferret ran up to the gate of his kennel and looked down to watch us pass. He made a funny chattering noise that was not a bark or a growl or a whimper.

At another stack of cages, Maggie Rose stopped. She put me down on the ground so that I could see into the bottom cage. I pressed my nose up to the gate.

I smelled a familiar smell.

There were two cats inside. Young ones. Small. A boy and a girl. I'd smelled them before, on my girl's shirt. Now they were right here in front of me!

One had stripes. The other had blotchy spots all over. Stripes was the boy. Blotchy was the girl. Stripes retreated into a box with his wide eyes on me, but Blotchy came cautiously over to the gate to touch noses. Her fur bristled out from her body a little, and I could smell that she was nervous. I wagged to let her know that I was friendly.

"See the kittens, Lily?" Maggie Rose whispered.

Stripes and Blotchy smelled a lot like cats, but they weren't cats, exactly. They were baby cats, the way puppies were baby dogs.

"Aren't they cute kittens?"

Kittens, I decided, was what Blotchy and Stripes were called. Kittens. Baby cats.

"Okay, guys?" my girl whispered. "Okay! Mom and Amelia say that you and Lily might hurt each other, but Lily is a rescue dog. She wouldn't hurt *anybody*. I have to prove it to them. So we're going to do this, okay?"

Maggie Rose took a deep breath and opened the pen.

13

When Maggie Rose opened the door so I could meet the kittens, I did not charge straight into the cage. I remembered how I did not like it when my brothers used to do that. They'd run right at me and bowl me over before I was ready to play.

Instead, I eased slowly up to Blotchy. She opened her mouth wide. I could see her sharp white teeth. I wondered if I should politely sniff her butt in greeting, as Missy the dog had taught me.

"Oh," Maggie Rose whispered nervously. "Maybe . . ."

I yawned, just like Blotchy. Then I sat down and stretched my neck to sniff at Blotchy's face. Her breath smelled very interesting! Meaty and fishy! I liked it! I wagged my tail.

Blotchy sniffed back, and then suddenly she pushed her face hard against my cheek. It almost shoved me right over! How could such a tiny thing push so hard?

She did it again, with the other side of her face. A funny rumbling sound came from deep in her throat. But it was not a growl. I could tell she was friendly.

I licked her face. She shook her head in surprise. Now her fur was wet.

Then something sharp stabbed at my tail!

I yelped in surprise and spun around. Behind me, Stripes leaped away on stiff legs. He'd crept up behind me and pounced on my tail!

Now he was running away!

Obviously, he wanted to play Chase Me!

He should have bowed in front of me before jumping on my tail like that, but it was all right. I was ready to play, though the cage we were in wasn't nearly as large as my dog pen.

I pursued Stripes back to his box, and he jumped up on top of it and let out a funny sound from a wide-open mouth—a hiss. What strange noises cats made.

Blotchy crouched down low, wiggled her rump, and pounced at me, grabbing my back foot with her claws.

Oh! Wrestle? We were playing Wrestle now?

I flopped down on Blotchy and rolled over. She batted at my ear. I mouthed at her leg. But I was careful not to bite, and she kept her claws gentle. They pricked my leg, but they didn't hurt.

She understood Wrestle.

"See?" Maggie Rose said softly. "I told them you wouldn't hurt the kittens."

Stripes leaped down from his box and landed on Blotchy's rump, and she sprang up and whirled around in midair. I wished I could do that! She chased her brother around the small cage, and I helped out by following her, until we all ended up in a heap in the middle of the kennel, gently playing. Blotchy suddenly started licking my ears and head with her strong, raspy pink tongue.

Did she think she was my mother?

Maggie Rose had both hands over her mouth to stifle her laughter, but it still slipped out in giggles around her fingers. "Silly Lily, you're so sweet!" she said as I shook my head so that Blotchy would stop licking me. "Come on back. Maybe that's enough for one day."

She reached in and pulled me out of the kitten kennel. Blotchy switched to washing Stripes's face until he batted her on the nose and darted over to get a drink from the water bowl.

Maggie Rose shut the gate to the kittens' kennel. Then she set me down in front of the stack of cages next to the kittens.

Freddie the ferret was already standing by his gate,

his tiny noise quivering, his whole long, slender body alert. I looked up at him, and he stared down at me.

"Lily, don't ever tell anybody about this," my girl said to me, very softly.

She opened the gate.

For a moment, Freddie sniffed cautiously at the air outside his kennel. I wagged. Then he slithered out, gripping the wires with his claws, and climbed down the outside of the cages and landed at my feet.

Freddie didn't run anything like my brothers with their big clumsy paws, or like Blotchy and Stripes with their featherlight movements. Freddie *flowed*. He was quick and smooth, dashing past me, racing along the rows of cages. Brewster barked, startled. Oscar meowed. Stripes and Blotchy mewed.

I chased.

Of course that's what we were doing, wasn't it? We were playing Chase Me! And just like the kittens, Freddie didn't quite know the rules. He didn't know to bow down or to look back over his shoulder to tell me to follow.

But I knew to run after him, anyway. Anything moving that quickly *needed* to be chased!

I couldn't get close to him! It was impossible. Freddie darted faster and faster. He switched directions so quickly that I nearly fell trying to keep up. He swarmed up and down cages and flashed across the wires and dropped down and raced out into the dog kennel area and then, just as quickly, raced back. Maggie Rose was starting to get nervous; I could tell.

"Don't go too far, Freddie!" she called anxiously.

I decided she wanted me to catch Freddie. I would do it! I would do anything for my girl!

Suddenly, Freddie doubled back on his own tracks again. One second, he was racing forward; the next, he was headed in the other direction! I tried to stop, skidding on the slick floor, my legs splaying.

Freddie halted at Brewster's cage and chittered through the bars at him. Brewster barked back, wagging. He wanted to play Chase Me, too. He wanted it very badly.

"Shhh, Brewster! Don't bark," Maggie Rose whispered. Brewster and I looked at her, wondering what she wanted.

I shook myself and prepared to follow Freddie some more. The ferret turned in a circle in front of Brewster's cage, almost as if he were teasing the big dog. I ran forward and jumped on Freddie. He couldn't get away this time!

We rolled over and over. At one point, Freddie nipped me on my nose. It didn't hurt much, though. And I was having much too good of a time to stop.

I jumped up and seized Freddie by the neck. Maggie Rose let out a little gasp. "Lily!" she cried out.

I wanted to reassure Maggie Rose, but I was busy. I dragged Freddie down the hallway. His long black-and-white body was limp in my mouth as if he were a puppy and I were a mother dog.

"Lily, no!" Maggie Rose called.

I looked up at her in surprise. No? Freddie took advantage of my confusion and wiggled out of my mouth. My turn to run! His turn to do Chase Me!

But the ferret surprised me. He didn't run after me. Instead, he jumped up on the wire gate of the cage that held Stripes and Blotchy, clinging to it with his claws. Both kittens retreated to their box.

I was learning about being a ferret. Freddie ran differently from how I did, he wasn't good at Chase Me, and he could climb as well as any squirrel! I watched in wonder as Freddie swarmed over the wires and ran across the top of the cages. I put my paws up on the door of the kitten cage and yipped. Now Stripes and Blotchy were mewing at me!

Freddie paused at the very top of the tower of cages. He looked at me over his shoulder. And then he wiggled down behind the stack, slipping easily into a crack between it and the wall behind.

He was gone. I couldn't see him anymore.

"Oh no!" Maggie Rose gasped. "Oh no. Freddie! Freddie! Come back! Please come back!"

I didn't understand what was going on. Where was Freddie? Was Chase Me over?

Maggie Rose darted to the stack of cat cages and grabbed hold of the wires and pulled. But every crate was connected to the cage on either side of it, and the whole row together was too heavy for my girl to move. Freddie remained hidden behind the cages, though I could still smell him easily enough.

My girl was breathing in quick gasps and sniffing hard. I could sense her fear and worry. Something was very wrong! But I didn't know what it was.

I whimpered to tell Maggie Rose that I was worried, too. We could be worried together.

"Lily!" she cried. "This is all my fault. What if he gets stuck back there? What if he can't get out?"

My girl sat down and grabbed me. She plopped me into her lap. Her hands were squeezing me a little too tightly, but I didn't mind very much. I could tell she needed me.

"Oh, Lily, there's a pipe back there that leads outside! I saw it once. I asked Mom about it; it's a drain. Ferrets love to explore. What if Freddie thinks it's a tunnel and crawls into it? He could end up outside. And he doesn't know how to live outside! Freddie might die, Lily!" Maggie Rose wailed.

My girl kept saying Freddie's name. Clearly, whatever was happening had to do with Freddie hiding from us. I'd better fix that right away.

I wiggled off Maggie Rose's lap and hurried over to the stack of cages where I'd last seen the ferret. When I climbed around behind them, I could see the crack between the cages and the wall.

Freddie was skinnier than I was. I couldn't force my body into that crack. I could barely push my nose in.

I could not see the ferret, but I could still smell him squeezed into the tight space. His wild animal odor was very clear. I whined a little. When I whined to my mother, she always came to find me. Maybe Freddie would do the same thing.

I heard a rustling noise. There was some movement, and then something tickled my nose. Whiskers! Small black eyes blinked at me from between the cages and the wall.

"There you are," Maggie Rose murmured. "Please come out, Freddie! Please!"

The ferret raised his nose, twitching it at me. I wondered if he was going to climb back behind the cages or come out to play.

"*Please*," Maggie Rose urged again.

14

I backed up, giving the ferret more room, and Freddie wiggled out from the crack. I sniffed him. He smelled dusty. He sniffed me back.

More Chase Me?

"Oh, Lily, good dog," Maggie Rose whispered. "Just come here so Freddie will follow you. Lily, come. Lily, please. Lily, come and see me."

Maggie Rose was saying my name a lot. I decided that she must need me. I trotted joyfully to her and licked the hand she was holding out.

Freddie scampered behind me. I was right! He was ready to run after me now!

But Maggie Rose seemed to think that playtime was at an end. She reached out for Freddie and snatched him up. He chattered at me and tried to twist himself out of my girl's hands, but she held him firmly and carried him to his cage. She put him in and shut the door.

Then she sat down on the floor and trembled, the way Missy the dog had trembled. I dashed to her and climbed into her lap. I didn't know why we couldn't play more, but Maggie Rose obviously needed a puppy right now, needed me more than ever. I pushed at her hands with my nose until she remembered to pet me. I could feel her calming down as she stroked my back and rubbed my neck. There, I was getting better at helping her! The fear was going away.

After Maggie Rose stopped shaking, she picked me up and carried me into my own kennel. She sat down next to my mother. It was very nice. Maggie Rose, my mother, and me, all cuddled together in our pen.

"I'll never, never do that again, Lily," she said softly. "That was wrong."

My mother sniffed at my girl's face, and I sniffed at my mother.

"But I was right about one thing. You were meant to help rescue animals. You saved the deer, and you calmed Missy down, and you got Freddie to come back. Dad says Mom is doing what she was always meant to do. How can I show them that it's the same for you? That you were meant to be here? They won't listen to me. They want you to live with someone else. Oh, Lily. I don't know what I'll do when they take you away from me."

Now my girl was as sad as she had ever been. After a little bit, she lay down on the dog bed. Her face was wet. My mother gently licked my girl's cheeks.

It reminded me of how my mother used to lick me when I was very small. Then she would pick me up by the skin on the back of my neck, the way I had just been carrying Freddie.

Her mouth was so very gentle when she did this that I was never afraid. I always knew she was taking me somewhere safe. That's what mothers do. I watched, but my mother didn't pick Maggie Rose up by the back of the neck.

I licked my girl's cheek, too. The wetness tasted salty.

It had been a very busy day so far! I wanted to just lie still for a bit of rest. I wiggled myself under my girl's chin, and my mother lay down along my girl's back, curling up with her the way she often curled up with me and my brothers. Maggie Rose's breathing slowed, and, before long, my mother drifted into sleep. I closed my eyes.

We all took a nice nap together—my girl, my mother, and me. It was the best nap I ever had, warm and safe and full of love.

When I woke up, Mom was standing there, gazing

down at the three of us. She was smiling, but she looked sad, too. She eased open the door and came into the kennel. I tapped my tail on the floor, which woke up my mother, who wagged as well. Mom sat down on the floor next to us and gently touched Maggie Rose's arm.

Maggie Rose stirred and opened her eyes.

"Hello, sweetie," Mom said. "Nice sleep?"

Maggie Rose nodded. She sat up and pulled me into her lap.

"Honey," Mom said after a few moments. "I know you love this little dog. But you've played with lots of dogs in the shelter, and you've always been happy when they've gotten adopted. Why is Lily so different?"

Maggie Rose looked down at me. I wagged.

"Because she's like me," she said in a voice so soft Mom leaned a little closer to hear it.

"Like you? What do you mean?" Mom asked. Her tone was as gentle as my mother's tongue. Maybe that's how human mothers lick their young ones—with words.

"We're both runts," Maggie Rose explained.

"Oh, honey," Mom answered.

"We are, Mom. I'm the shortest girl in my class at school, and Lily is the smallest one in the litter. And she had big brothers, too. Just like me."

"I see," Mom said, nodding.

"And I just . . . love her, Mom. I just do. And she loves me."

Mom nodded again. "I can see that. But, honey, you have to believe me when I tell you this—you'll love other dogs in your life. Lily is very special, but all dogs are special. And I have good news. We just finished processing an application, and Lily's mother is being adopted! Isn't that wonderful? I'm going to take her to her new home right now."

"But Lily will be all alone," Maggie Rose objected.

"No, hon, when I take her mother, she won't be lonely because she'll have you," Mom answered, still in that gentle voice. "And then she'll have a person of her own very soon. A man has applied and been accepted. He just asked for a few days to think about it, which makes me glad. Adopting a dog is a big, important decision, something no one should rush into."

Mom took out a leash and clipped it onto my mother's collar. No treats were given. Then she tugged on the leash gently.

"Come, sweetie," she said. "Come with me. You're going to your new forever home."

My mother got up and shook herself. She looked at me, still in Maggie Rose's lap. Then she followed Mom out of the kennel. Mom shut the door behind her and walked out of sight, but my mother halted. I saw the leash on my mother's collar lift up and go tight, and I pictured Mom at the end of it, pulling gently.

My mother was staring at me, and I was staring at my mother. She wagged.

"Come on, girl," I heard Mom urge kindly.

With one last look at me, my mother turned away and vanished from my view.

I was very confused. I wiggled out of my girl's lap and went to the kennel door and sniffed. I could tell my mother's scent was following Mom farther and farther away.

I whined. She always came when I whined.

But this time, she did not come.

I whined again, louder. Maybe she hadn't heard me the first time.

"Oh, Lily!" Maggie Rose said mournfully.

She picked me up and held me tightly. She petted me and talked to me. Her cheeks were wet again, and they had that salty taste. She was so, so sad. She rocked me gently back and forth.

"It'll be okay. It'll be okay," she told me.

I was glad that Maggie Rose was so close. But I wished my mother were there, too. Being held by my girl, my nose filled with the scent of my mother still heavy on our bed, brought back the sense of peace and love I had felt while we had all been napping together. At that moment, I had been as happy as I had ever been.

But now my girl was sad, and I could not just lie in her lap recalling a wonderful nap. I was her puppy! I had work to do! I climbed off her and pranced over to the door, gazing at Maggie Rose expectantly.

"Do you want out?" She crawled over on her hands and knees like a dog, reached up, and opened the gate.

I trotted confidently down the hallway.

"Lily?" my girl called.

I found the towel that the furry-faced man had played with. I could still smell his hands on it. I grabbed it in my mouth and proudly took it to Maggie Rose, shaking it vigorously. Surely this would cheer her up! It was a towel!

"You silly dog," she said. I heard *dog* and figured I just about had her. I danced close, allowing the towel to touch one of her crossed legs. When she didn't grab it, I shook it and then acted as if I hadn't meant to drop it into her lap. It had just happened. Oops!

She picked it up, and I lunged—yes! But when I pulled, she released it without resistance. I was dismayed to realize she was still sad despite having a towel with a puppy attached.

After a while, Mom returned and spoke to Maggie Rose. "Time to go, sweetie."

It had been a strange day—fun, then scary, then cozy, then sad. I hoped it would be fun again soon. I hoped my mother would come back, and she and Maggie Rose and I could be together and take another nap in the dog bed.

Mom and Maggie Rose left. This had happened many times before, but never when I was in the kennel by myself. I sniffed, trying to find my mother on the air currents.

After a while, Amelia turned out most of the lights and *she* left. It was dark. It was very quiet. And it was so lonely. I had never been by myself in my kennel at night. I had never imagined how alone I would feel. It hurt, a hollow ache in my chest. This had *never* happened before!

I could smell Freddie and Brewster and Oscar and Stripes and Blotchy. I could smell my brothers, although their scents were starting to fade. I could smell my mother.

All alone, I lay on the bed that smelled like my family. I whined and whimpered a *lot*, but no one came to be with me.

It was the worst night of my life.

In the morning, lights popped on, and Amelia brought me food in bowls and fresh water. I was so happy to see her that I charged up to her the moment she opened my kennel door, licking her pants and shoes and panting anxiously up into her face and trying to let her know how awful, how very awful, the night had been. Where was my mother? Where was Maggie Rose? Where was everybody?

"There, there, Lily!" Amelia petted me gently. "It's going to be okay. It won't be long now."

Later, after breakfast, my girl came. Maggie Rose! I flung myself at her, and she held me until all the loneliness of the night before had been forgotten.

My mother was still gone. My brothers were still gone. But Maggie Rose was there. And I loved Maggie Rose. As long as we were together, I would never be lonely.

Mom came to the gate of our kennel and stood there, looking in.

"I have some news, Maggie Rose," she said.

Maggie Rose looked up hopefully.

"Lily's new owner has decided he wants her," she said. "I'll be taking her there tomorrow."

My girl's smile fell away. The sadness, which was always lurking in her like a shadow, came forward and took over her mood completely.

Mom came into the kennel and tried to hug my girl and talk to her in those words that were like a mother dog licking her puppy, but Maggie Rose did not want to be held. She did not want words. She turned away from Mom, her face tight.

At last, Mom patted her shoulder and left.

Maggie Rose held me and cried and cried. I did my best to fix things. I licked her chin and her salty face. I nuzzled my head under her arm so I'd be as close to her as I could. I told her without words that I was her dog and that she didn't need to be so sad when I was with her.

But none of it helped. All that day, Maggie Rose was as sad as I'd been all night long.

Why couldn't I make her happy?

15

At the end of that sad day, Maggie Rose left with Mom, and I spent a second night all alone. Another one! When would this end?

I was frantic with joy when my girl came to see me early in the morning. I tried to tell her with my whimpers and my kisses how happy I was that she was back and things were normal! I forgave her because she was my girl. As I nibbled on her hands, I loved her so much that my jaws were quivering.

She was still sad, though! I could not understand it. It made sense to be unhappy when we were apart. But when we were together, why would she be anything but overjoyed? What was I doing wrong?

I tried rolling on my back and racing around in

circles and jumping up to lick her face—all the puppy tricks I had. None of it seemed to work.

My girl slipped a collar around my neck and attached a leash to it. Treat! Then she took me into the hallway.

But we didn't stop and play there, as I'd expected. Maggie Rose led me through a door to Outside. I squatted and was rewarded with a treat. I was so happy about the way my girl understood that peeing and treats went together. This arrangement was so fixed in my mind that I was starting to feel that Outside was the right place for squatting, and it felt wrong and strange to do it in my dog kennel. I would hold back until we were here, Outside.

After figuring out that there would be no more treats, I put my nose down to the grass, which smelled fresh and alive and like all the things that had walked on it and peed on it. It had bugs and sticks hidden in it. And underneath it was rich, fragrant dirt.

Then Maggie Rose picked me up. I was not done sniffing and digging and exploring, but I was excited to see where we were going next. My girl tucked me tightly under one arm and slid into a big van, one with a ceiling so high that Mom could stand up in it if she'd wanted to.

Maggie Rose sat in a backseat, holding me in her lap. She took a leash from the wall and stretched it across her lap, then snapped it into a buckle that was next to her leg instead of around her neck. Nobody gave her a treat for doing this. I guessed that the rules for leashes were different for girls than for dogs. Mom climbed up front, sitting behind a big wheel that she held with her hands.

The van smelled even more interesting than the dirt! So many animals had been here. My mother! My mother had been in this van! I squirmed out of Maggie Rose's arms and sniffed the seats. I sniffed the floor that was covered in rough carpet. I could smell that my mother had been nervous, but not too scared. Where had she gone?

And others from my dog family had been here. I thought I caught a faint whiff of White-Tail-Brother buried deep in the cushions of the seat where Maggie Rose was sitting. Brewster had definitely been here as well, and not too long ago.

The van suddenly gave a lurch, and I staggered. Maggie Rose picked me up and held me on her lap. "Here we go, Lily," she said.

We were moving, and this time I hadn't started out in a cat bed!

I braced my back feet on Maggie Rose's lap and my front feet on a slippery glass window and stared outside in amazement. Things were flying past us faster than I could run—trees and other cars, signs and posts and wires, bushes and buildings, people walking. Some of the people had dogs with them. I had never known that the world was so big and so busy and so full!

My girl pressed something, and the window moved a bit. Cool air rushed in through a gap between the top of the window and its frame, packed so full of smells that I almost wet on my girl, I was so excited. I pressed my nose to the gap and sniffed and sniffed and sniffed.

This was so much better than being in a cat bed!

There was something familiar about the wonderful mix of odors blowing in. When had I smelled something like that before? Oh yes, when I'd lived with my mother and brothers before the shelter. That had been a cold, dark time, but interesting smells like this had wafted past my nose most days. Then we'd gone to live in our kennel, and there we'd mostly been able to smell ourselves, plus the other animals, the not-dogs, and people like Maggie Rose and Mom and Amelia.

But now! Now I had Maggie Rose to snuggle with and all the wonderful odors to fill my nose. I whapped my tail back and forth, swatting Maggie Rose's chest and arms. This was amazing! This was the best adventure ever!

But Maggie Rose didn't seem to think so. I could

still feel her sadness soaking into me. I suddenly felt like a bad dog for being so thrilled and excited while my girl suffered. I dropped my paws off the glass and put them on my girl's chest, staring into her eyes, willing her to laugh and be happy that there was a puppy in her lap.

From her seat up front, Mom was talking. "This is going to be a wonderful home for Lily. The man who's adopting her is a radio disc jockey, and that means he's only at work for half a day in the morning. The rest of the time he's home and can stay with Lily. She'll have plenty of company. She'll have a great life."

Maggie Rose put her head down and buried her face in my fur. She didn't answer. I dug my head in under hers and pushed, licking her face.

It wasn't working.

Suddenly, a funny burst of noise came from the seat next to Mom! My ears perked up to hear it. Mom turned the wheel, and the van moved to the side of the road and stopped. She put a small black box to her ear. "Hello?"

Then Mom talked for a while more. She was quiet for a bit, nodding, and then she started talking again. People do strange stuff sometimes, and all a puppy can do is wait for things to make sense again.

Mom put the black box down.

"We need to make a detour, Maggie Rose," she said. "That was Amelia. She just got a call. There's a duplex near here where some people moved out more than a month ago. The landlord just went in to clean out the vacant apartment and found a bunch of cats living there. Probably a mom with kittens. It's that time of year. We'll have to go and get them. It shouldn't take too long."

Maggie Rose snuggled her face back into my fur again.

"I wish it would take forever," she whispered to me mournfully. "Then we could stay together, Lily."

The van rolled along for a while longer and then stopped. Maggie Rose slid out, still holding me. Mom jumped out, too. She went to the back of the van, opened up a door, and took out two plastic boxes with wire gates on the front. They looked like small kennels, but with handles on the top so that they could be carried.

There was a building nearby with two front doors. A man came out of one of those doors. He closed the door behind him, but I heard barking. I sniffed. Dogs lived behind that door. Two of them.

"Thanks for coming," the man said. He wore a grubby shirt and a pair of jeans with dirt ground into the knees. "I haven't been into the place since the last tenants left. This morning, I was going to get it cleaned

150

up and ready for the new people, and in one of the bed-
rooms upstairs I found a bunch of cats! Couldn't believe it!"

"Cats or kittens?" Mom asked.

The man shrugged. "Beats me. I didn't look too
closely, just shut the door so they couldn't get out. Some
were small, so sure, kittens, maybe. I don't know that
much about cats. I've got dogs. Cats and dogs don't get
along, ever."

"That's not true," Maggie Rose objected softly. "Lily
loves cats. Kittens, too. She gets along with everybody."

The man shrugged again. "Well, I wouldn't take a
puppy in there. Want me to hang on to yours while you
take care of the cats?"

Maggie Rose hugged me more tightly. "No!" she said
firmly.

The man sniffed. "Suit yourself," he replied.

Mom sighed. "Sorry, she didn't mean to be rude.
Maggie Rose? What do you have to say for yourself?"

My girl looked down at the ground, so I did, too. I
didn't see anything to look at but was ready to get down
and roll around if she wanted to. "I'm sorry," Maggie
Rose muttered.

"No problem," the man replied.

Mom touched my girl's shoulder. "Maggie Rose,
come with me. But keep an eye on Lily until we know
what we're dealing with."

We went through the other door, which did not have dogs behind it. Mom walked ahead, carrying her small kennels. Maggie Rose followed behind her, carrying me.

Once we were inside the door, Mom shut it behind us. At once, I could smell cats.

Cats! When I'd played with Stripes and Blotchy, Maggie Rose had giggled. I realized I knew how to make her happy after all! I'd find these cats and play with them!

"Why did you say 'until we know what we're dealing with,' Mom?" Maggie Rose queried.

Mom glanced at the closed door. "He said he couldn't tell the difference between cats and kittens. This close to the mountains, I don't know what kind of animal he might have found. One time, a woman had us come out to rescue cats in her barn and they were bobcats!"

"What?" Maggie Rose exclaimed. "What did you do?"

Mom smiled. "Called your father, of course. He came out and relocated them to a place where they were safe."

I wiggled until my girl set me down. The floor was made of slippery wood. I didn't let that bother me, though. I scrambled and slid from corner to corner, sniffing hard. Where were those cats?

Mom and my girl kept walking, so I scampered to keep up. Then I halted.

Stairs.

Mom climbed on the first step, then the second, then the next, moving up. Maggie Rose did the same. I'd never seen people do anything like that!

Well, I would just have to follow. The first stair was tall! Almost as tall as I was! It was hard work to jump up and put my front feet on its surface. I hoped they wouldn't all be like this!

Then I tried to heave my back feet up behind me.

Impossible! My back feet slipped off the stair, and my front feet could not hold on. I scrabbled at the wood with my claws before I flopped back to the floor.

Maggie Rose and Mom were already nearly at the top. There were doors up there, and new rooms, and the smell of cats was even stronger.

I yipped in frustration, and my girl turned around.

"Oh, Lily!" she exclaimed. She came down to get me.

It felt so, so good to be back in her arms. I hoped I would never again be separated from Maggie Rose.

Mom was standing in front of a closed door. The smell of cats wafted out from under it. They were inside there! Lots of them, young ones, by their scents.

We were going to have such fun!

"Keep hold of Lily," Mom said, pulling a pair of thick

leather gloves over her hands. They went up to her elbows.

I wagged to hear my name and because I was going to get to play with kittens again very soon.

Mom opened the door.

16

I was so excited to see that door open that I could not possibly remain in my girl's arms, no matter how secure it felt. I wiggled and squirmed and pushed with my back feet. Maggie Rose gasped with alarm and shifted her grip, but I gave one last twist and jumped to the floor.

Kittens!

"Lily, no!" Maggie Rose fell to her knees, grabbing for me, but she was too late for a grab and too late for that *no* word. I darted right through Mom's legs. Her fingers brushed my back as she reached for me, but I did not stop. I ran straight into that room, where I knew the cats were waiting for me.

Maybe a puppy alone wasn't enough to lift my girl's sadness, but a puppy playing with kittens would surely put a smile on her face!

"Lily!" Mom called sternly.

Sometimes people will speak in a certain tone of voice. When they do, it's best to ignore them, because that kind of voice never leads to any fun. It's especially important to ignore them when there is a new cat family to meet!

The mother cat, black all over, was sitting on a bare mattress on the bed. When I bounded in, she leaped to her feet with the most astonishing sound I'd ever heard. It was sort of a snarl and sort of a wail. Her ears were flat against her head, and with her fur fluffed out all over, she appeared twice my size! Her mouth was open wide, and she hissed, showing all her teeth. They looked very sharp.

From up on the bed beside the angry mother, there came a sound of frantic, high-pitched mewing. Kittens leaped off the mattress and raced in all directions, even faster than Stripes and Blotchy ran when we'd played Chase Me. A gray kitten disappeared under the dresser, two with yellowish stripes dived beneath the bed, and a little black one disappeared, though I could not see where. On the bed, a white kitten backed up her mother by hissing ferociously at me and showing me all her tiny teeth.

"Maggie Rose! Shut the door so none of the kittens get out! Quick!" Mom said. "And then get Lily!"

I jumped up and put my front paws on the edge of the mattress, wagging furiously. The mother cat and the baby cat were still angry, even though I was clearly just trying to play. I glanced over my shoulder for help as Mom slowly approached the bed.

"Easy, sweetie, we're here to take care of you," she told the ferocious mother cat.

Maggie Rose shut the door and came toward me. I dashed to the opposite side of the bed from Mom and put my front feet up there, wagging. I was sure that the cats would see that I was a good playmate. My ears were up, my tail was high, and I gave a friendly yip. They'd understand that I was no threat, and once we started to wrestle, my girl would laugh and want to play, too.

The mother cat did not seem to like the idea of Mom or my girl getting close to the bed. This is the frustrating thing about cats; they live with people but don't care about them as much as dogs do. I could tell by her stiff, unfriendly posture that it was not important to the mother cat whether Maggie Rose was happy or not.

The mother retreated, still hissing, and fluffed herself up even bigger. How did she do that? My fur could go up a bit around my neck and shoulders if I wanted to look fierce, but hers could bristle all over her body!

I jumped but fell back on the floor with a plop. This bed was even harder to climb up on than a stair!

The mother cat was moving away from me, right toward Mom. She seemed more worried about a puppy than people. In one quick movement, Mom put both of her gloved hands around the cat's body.

The mother yowled and fought, but Mom held her tightly and sighed with relief. "Okay, I'll get her in a cage and take it downstairs," she told Maggie Rose. "The kittens will be calmer if they can't hear her. See if you can start catching them."

Mom hauled the struggling mother cat out of the room, closing the door quickly behind her. The white kitten on the bed was still hissing and spitting at me.

Suddenly, Maggie Rose was tense all over. I looked up at her in surprise. Weren't we playing?

She didn't seem sad. She seemed excited. "Lily, this is our last chance," she whispered to me. "Help with the kitten. We'll show Mom what you can do!"

She picked me up and dumped me on the bed.

I understood now that this kitten wasn't furious like the mother. She was frightened, just as Missy had been frightened. But I'd shown Missy that I was not scary. I could do the same thing here.

First I crouched down on the bed so I would not tower over the kitten. Then I squirmed toward her on my belly. The kitten stopped hissing, but she backed away from me, confused. Maggie Rose swept toward her and scooped her up in her hands.

"There, there, it's okay," she whispered, cuddling the kitten close to her chest and stroking its fur.

That kitten was no longer available to play with, but there were plenty of others! I was happy to see my girl holding a kitten—she seemed less sad now. My plan to cheer her up was working.

Excited, I leaped down to the floor and poked my nose under the bed. A tiny yellowish paw with even tinier claws shot out at me. I jumped back, shaking my head and sneezing. This was not a mean kitten or an angry kitten—he wanted to play! I could tell by how softly the paw had landed on my snout. I thrust my nose toward the space under the mattress again, sniffing eagerly. A yellowish face peeked out.

"Good, Lily!" Maggie Rose sang, and she leaned down and swept up one yellowish kitten. When a yellow sister stuck her head out to see what was going on, my girl grabbed her as well. She plopped them both on the bed next to the white kitten, who was no longer hissing. They sniffed each other, probably marveling that they had met a puppy.

The gray kitten under the dresser was meowing frantically as if it couldn't get out. My girl lay down flat on the floor and reached beneath the piece of furniture.

Her hand came out clutching a kitten, which she took to the bed, too.

There was now a pile of kittens up there! I wagged up at them because the white kitten was staring down at me and the two yellowish ones were wandering over the mattress, mewing. Maggie Rose set the gray one down among them. Then she reached down for me.

"Okay, Lily," she said. "Help them not to be scared. Mom will see you're a rescue dog. Lily, you can do this!"

She put me down on the bed. Kittens scattered and squeaked or sat and stared.

I sat, too, and stared back. These were kittens like Stripes and Blotchy, but I wasn't sure if they all wanted to play like Stripes and Blotchy had. Would they puff up and yowl and hiss like the angry mother cat?

No, they wouldn't. They seemed curious about me now that I was sitting down. The white one and one of the yellowish ones came hesitantly forward on skinny legs to examine me.

I stretched out my nose. They sniffed. I sniffed.

Their fear was leaving them. One of them nuzzled at my cheek, emitting a tiny not-barking sound. The gray one came toward me, unsure, ready to run.

I licked his face. He fell back in surprise, his bright eyes blinking. One of his sisters pounced on him. They were playing!

I poked my nose between them, hoping they would let me play, too.

I could sense my girl standing at the edge of the bed, watching eagerly. Clearly, I'd been right all along. Watching her puppy play with kittens was the secret to pushing away her sadness.

The little white kitten crouched down. Her rump stuck up. It wiggled. It wasn't exactly like a bow that a dog would make if he or she wanted a game, but it was close. Was she telling me she wanted to play with me?

Yes, she was! There wasn't much room on the mattress for Chase Me, though I was certainly willing. But instead of running away so I could run after her, she leaped and landed with both front paws around one of mine. She wrestled with my foot and gnawed on it, but her jaws were too weak to really hurt. I picked up my paw and shook it. She tumbled off.

Sitting on the squishy mattress with three paws down and one paw up made me wobble. If I fell, I'd be lying down, and the kittens could climb over me just the way my brothers used to. They might like that. My brothers certainly had. I flopped over, wagging, my tail tapping the bed.

A yellowish kitten and the gray one came to sniff at my face. The gray one batted at my ear.

The other yellowish one leaped nimbly up and

walked along my side. Her tiny claws pricked and tickled.

The white kitten sprang at me to seize my paw again and wrestle with it more.

"Good dog, Lily!" my girl praised. "They're not scared anymore!"

I could tell now that these kittens were even younger than Stripes and Blotchy. That meant I had to be gentle with them. My brothers had never been gentle with me when they wanted to play, but my mother had been. When she wrapped her body around mine or picked me up by the skin on the back of my neck, she'd always been careful not to hurt me.

I could be like that. I could be careful with the kittens.

The door opened. I glanced over and saw the man who smelled like two different dogs. "What in the world is going on here?" he demanded.

Maggie Rose straightened her posture with a jerk and a small gasp. I jumped up, concerned. Kittens rolled in every direction, mewing.

What was the matter with my girl? Did she need me?

17

The kittens decided that, because I was standing still and staring at my girl, they should attack me from all sides. But for the moment, I wasn't playing.

"No, no, don't be alarmed; I'm sorry if I startled you," the man said softly. "Your mom told me it would be okay if I came in to see. Look how cute they are! And they sure do seem to like your puppy—never seen anything like that in my life."

Maggie Rose relaxed, and I wagged. "Lily makes friends with all animals," she said.

The gray kitten leaped at my ear and began to gnaw on it. I shook my head, and we both fell over. More kittens pounced from every side. As we wrestled, I smelled

Mom, and a moment later she was in the room. "Good work, Maggie Rose," Mom praised.

"It was Lily," my girl replied. "Look, Mom, look what she's—"

But Mom interrupted her. She was holding one of those kennels in her hands. "Okay, let's get them in here while they're all nice and calm."

"Mom—" Maggie Rose tried again.

"Not right now, Maggie Rose!"

My girl and Mom picked up the mewing, squirming kittens and put them one by one into the little kennel. I decided this must mean they would be going home with us! I was thrilled; I loved having kittens around. Blotchy and Stripes would be so excited!

The man stood by the door and watched. "Cute little things. What's going to happen to them?" he asked.

"We can always find a home for kittens," Mom said. "Who doesn't love a kitten?"

"You think maybe I could have one?" he asked. "I never saw anything so cute."

"Well, sure," Mom replied. "This is your property. I suppose that means that technically they belong to you. But you said you have two dogs?"

"Yeah, Dusty and Beezo. But these little fellows seem to get along with dogs just fine."

"They do, but Lily's a puppy," Mom pointed out.

"A very special puppy," my girl chimed in. "She's a rescue dog!"

Mom smiled but kept talking to the man, not to my girl. "Plenty of dogs are just fine with cats, but we would want to be very careful to make sure Dusty and Beezo are gentle with them. It's easy for kittens to get hurt when they are so little. Have your dogs ever been around cats before?"

"Chased a couple now and again," the man replied. "We don't get a lot of cats around here."

"Well," Mom replied, "that doesn't sound very promising . . ."

"Gotcha," the man said. "Probably not the best idea after all. I wouldn't be a good person for a cat, anyway; I've never had one before. I'm pretty impressed with your pup there, though."

Mom nodded as Maggie Rose picked up the yellowish kitten, the last one left on the bed, and slipped her into the small kennel with her brothers and sisters. "It's because Lily's still a puppy that the kittens trusted her so quickly," Mom explained. "Young animals are usually seen as nonthreatening, even by other animals. It helps that Lily's so small. The kittens see her as just another baby like them."

"No," my girl corrected firmly, fastening the gate on the small kennel as the kittens mewed inside and stuck their little paws through the wires. "It's because Lily's a rescue dog. She just knows what to do when we find animals who need our help."

"Well, maybe," Mom said with another smile as she picked up the kennel full of complaining kittens. "Come on, let's get these babies outside."

The racket the kittens were making inside the kennel was so loud that I almost missed a panicky mew coming from a different place. There was a closet across the room, with the door propped open a tiny bit. I would have thought that gap between door and wall was too small for any animal to slip inside, but I'd seen the small gray kitten wiggle into a space beneath the dresser that was not any bigger.

"Come on, time to go," Mom said, and she and Maggie Rose headed for the door.

"Come, Lily!" Maggie Rose called. "Mom, I really want to ask you—"

"In the van, Maggie Rose. Okay?"

I jumped off the bed and hurried to the closet. I put my nose to the crack and could smell kitten inside there.

Small. Female. Frightened and alone.

I pushed at the door with my nose and scratched at it with a paw, but it was stuck. It didn't want to close all the way or open any farther.

"Come on, Lily," my girl urged, coming up behind me. She put her hands underneath my belly and scooped me up.

I whined. We should not leave the kitten behind! I knew that wasn't right. The kittens needed to be together, on the bed or in the small kennel. If one of them was by herself, she would feel as lonely and miserable as I'd felt for these last few nights alone in my bed.

But Maggie Rose didn't understand. She carried me out of the room and down the staircase. With every step down, I could sense that we were farther and farther away from the trapped kitten. "Stop squirming, Lily!" she said. "Okay, okay, you can get down!"

She set me down on the wooden floor at the foot of the stairs.

The man opened the door for Mom, who carried the small kennel full of mewing kittens outside.

My girl went out the door, too.

I hesitated. I knew I should follow my girl. I always wanted to be close to Maggie Rose. But the kitten was alone upstairs.

What should I do?

Maggie Rose would return for me, I knew. But that kitten hadn't come out of the closet. Maybe she *couldn't*. And even if she did, her mother cat and her littermates were gone. My girl and Mom and the man were gone.

There was only me.

I turned to face the stairs. I hadn't been able to climb them before, but the humans had. It couldn't be *impossible*.

I jumped up to get my front paws on the bottom step.

Then I put as much weight as I could on my front legs and tried to lift my back legs up onto the step as well. It was hard. My claws scrabbled at wood and paint. But at last all four paws were on the first step.

Now I just had to do that again.

And again.

Outside, I could hear Mom and my girl talking. "Maggie Rose, can you open the van door for me?" Mom asked. "Let's get these kittens inside. The mother will feel better once she can smell her babies."

"Mom . . . ," said Maggie Rose, hesitating.

The second step now. First front paws. Then back.

"Yes, what?"

I heard the van door opening.

My front paws slipped. I fell back to the first step.

"Didn't Lily do such a good job? Helping the kittens calm down?"

Mom sighed. "Please, Maggie Rose. Don't start."

I got back up and tried again. Front paws jumped. Back paws scrabbled. Pull . . . strain . . . and there! All my paws on step two.

"But, Mom, Lily is . . ." Her voice trailed off. "Where's Lily?" My girl's voice called for me. "Lily! Lily, where are you?"

I knew I should go to her . . . and I would. As soon

as I finished this job. I was starting to get better at the stairs. Another step, then another, then another. I was climbing!

I heard Maggie Rose's feet coming close to the door. Then I heard the door open. Oh no! She was coming to get me! I had to help the kitten!

I frantically heaved myself up several more steps. My legs were beginning to tire. This was hard!

"Lily! What are you doing, silly dog?" Maggie Rose started up the stairs after me.

I had to be quick! My legs were starting to tremble, but I still struggled up the last of the stairs, panting. I banged my chin on the floor of the hallway when I shoved my back feet off the final step, but I'd made it! It felt so good to be trotting on a level floor again.

"Lily! Come back!" Maggie Rose was more than halfway up the stairs now. I hurried to the bedroom where we'd found the kittens and their mother cat.

The door was still open. I ran straight up to the closet and stuck my nose into the gap between the door and the frame. The kitten was still in there. Still alone.

Still scared.

I barked. That made the kitten even more scared, so it was not the right thing to do. I'd better not bark again.

"Maggie Rose!" Mom called from downstairs. "Get Lily and come on!"

"I'm getting her, Mom!" Maggie Rose called back. Her feet were approaching from down the hallway now.

I pawed at the closet door. It didn't budge. Then I pushed my nose into the crack once more and shoved as hard as I could. I couldn't tell if the door moved or if my body just squished, but it worked. I was in!

"Lily!" Maggie Rose was at the bedroom door. "Lily, I saw you. What are you doing? Come out of there!" I heard my girl walking across the bedroom floor.

"Maggie Rose, where are you? What's going on?" Mom was climbing the stairs now.

Along the back wall of the closet was a stack of cardboard boxes. The kitten was behind them, just as Freddie had been behind the cages when we'd been playing Chase Me. But Freddie had been happy. This kitten was not happy. I could smell fear and misery.

I pushed my nose into the gap between a box and the wall. There was the kitten, huddled in a quivering ball of black fur. I nudged her with my nose. She only curled up tighter.

The kitten needed to leave this space. She could not stay here all alone.

"Lily, what are you doing? We have to go! Come on!" Grunting, Maggie Rose slid the closet door all the way open with a bang. The little kitten flinched.

This was a very tiny kitten. I was bigger than she was, just as my mother was bigger than I was.

I knew what to do with a tiny creature that needed to be somewhere else. Very gently, just as my mother used to do with me, I picked the kitten up by the loose skin at the back of her neck.

She did not struggle. She hung limply from my mouth like a ferret as I backed away from the boxes, toward my girl. I smelled Mom and knew she had entered the room behind Maggie Rose, but I stayed focused on the kitten in my mouth.

Maggie Rose gasped, raising a hand to her mouth. "*Lily,*" she breathed.

18

I held that little kitten as softly as my jaws would allow. My girl retreated into the bedroom, giving me room to turn around. I did it carefully. I did not want to startle the kitten or hurt her neck.

"Mom, look," Maggie Rose said softly. "Look what Lily did!"

I heard Mom draw in her breath. "Another kitten," she whispered. "In the closet? Oh, Maggie Rose. Oh, Lily. We almost left her here!"

"Mom, she would have starved!"

"You're right, honey." Mom nodded. "I should have thought to check to make sure there were no kittens hiding anywhere. It was my mistake."

I carried the kitten to my girl's feet and gently put her down. The kitten sat, looking around in a daze. Maggie Rose bent down and picked her up as tenderly as possible.

"Lily, good girl," she whispered as the scared kitten cuddled against her chest.

"Yes. Lily, you are a good, good dog," Mom said. She knelt and stroked me. "Such a good dog."

Feeling their love and hearing them both say *good dog* made me wag.

Maggie Rose gave the black kitten to Mom and picked me up to carry me back downstairs. I was relieved that I did not have to climb *down* those steps. Stairs were hard work!

"We'll drop off Lily and then get the cats back to the shelter," Mom said as we walked outside.

She put the black kitten into the kennel with her littermates, and Maggie Rose slid into the backseat with me. I was tired from all the excitement of playing with the kittens and climbing the stairs. I settled down for a nice doze on my girl's lap. This had been a fun adventure, but the best part of the whole day, of every day, was cuddling with Maggie Rose.

"Mom . . . ," Maggie Rose said as the van started to move.

"Honey, I know what you're about to say," Mom said.

"But can't you see what Lily did?" Maggie Rose pleaded. "She rescued that kitten! We never would have found it if Lily hadn't gone back. Mom, she saved it!"

"I know, Maggie Rose. I know. It was a lucky accident."

"She was born to be a rescue dog!"

I could feel Maggie Rose's anger and fear and sadness trembling through her. Why was she so upset? No kittens were in trouble anymore.

I sat up to stretch my head toward Maggie Rose's face. Her neck was as high as I could reach. I licked her under her chin. I just didn't know what else to do to make her happy. I felt like a bad puppy.

Maggie Rose didn't say anything more. Mom didn't say anything, either. The van drove.

I fell asleep even though Maggie Rose was sad once more. But when the van rocked to a stop, I woke at once, focused on my girl. Something was very wrong now.

Her heart was pounding, and her skin felt hot. Sadness was breaking in her, more painful and raw than anything I had ever felt. I simply did not know what to do to help her.

Mom climbed out and opened our door.

Snick. Leash on collar. Treat!

Sun and warm air and the scent of plants and trees flowed in on soft currents. I imagined playing in the Outside with my girl and hoped someone had thought

176

to bring a bouncy ball. That would make anyone happier!

"Well!" came a booming voice. I looked up and saw and smelled a man I had met before. He had a furry face and a big smile.

The man reached right in and picked me up, pulling me away from my girl in such a sudden motion that I had no warning before I was up in the air and nearly nose-to-nose with him. "It's a puppy delivery service!" he announced with a chuckle. "I can't tell you how much I appreciate you bringing me my new dog. Hello, Lily!"

Bewildered, I did the only thing I could think of, which was to lick the nose that was right there in front of me. My tongue briefly encountered some of the fur around his lip.

The man laughed. "This is going to be wonderful!" he declared. "I don't know why I waited this long!"

"Glad to do it," Mom replied. "And thank you for your generous contribution. We do have adoption fees, but if it weren't for donations, we couldn't do all the work we do. Mr. Mancuso, this is my daughter, Maggie Rose."

"Hello, Maggie."

"Maggie *Rose*," she muttered in unhappy tones.

"Oh. I see." Furry Face Man smiled. "Maggie *Rose*, I should have said. It's very nice to meet you."

Maggie Rose didn't say anything in return. Anger and hurt were jumping off her skin. I wriggled a little, hoping Furry Face would soon hand me back to my girl.

"Maggie Rose, please." Mom sighed. "I'm sorry, Mr. Mancuso, it's been a bit of a trying day so far. We were on our way here when we got a call about some abandoned kittens we had to rescue. That's why we're late."

"Call me Johnny. Did you say kittens? Could I see?"

The man carried me into the van. He was tall enough that his head almost touched the ceiling. He held me up to see the kittens, but I wasn't much impressed since I'd already spent so much time with them. "They are tiny," he gushed. "And so cute!"

Maggie Rose turned toward him with sudden energy. "You should have a kitten! Cats are much easier than a dog when you have to go to work every day. A puppy needs constant attention, but a cat can take care of itself! Plus you could take a kitten to work with you if you wanted and you would hardly know she was there!"

Mom put a hand out and touched my girl's shoulder.

"It's such important work, what you're doing," Furry Face replied, speaking to Mom. "You should come on my radio program sometime and talk about it. Folks need to understand how vital rescue is and why it's necessary."

We all climbed out into the sunshine. I took a deep whiff of air, ready to jump down and have some fun with Maggie Rose.

"I'd love to do that!" Mom exclaimed. "We're really trying to spread the word about how wrong it is to not spay and neuter pets. A single female can have as many as thirty kittens in a year. In a decade, she could have more than four thousand female kittens. And of course, if they go on to have their own babies, we'd be talking about fifty thousand kittens."

"Fifty thousand?" Furry Face whistled softly.

I looked around alertly. Playtime now? But he didn't seem to mean that.

"You're telling me that a female cat can have fifty thousand descendants in her lifetime?"

Mom shook her head. "No, not in her lifetime. In one decade, that one cat will result in fifty thousand kittens a *year*, if all the cats are allowed to breed freely. And the ones who are without a home will suffer. Disease, starvation, accidents with cars—there's so much that can happen to a homeless animal."

"I never knew any of that," said Furry Face. "Amazing."

"Lily does it, too," Maggie Rose said.

Still in the man's arms, I wagged. I loved it when my girl said my name.

"Does what? What do you mean?" Furry Face asked.

"She helps homeless kittens! She found the tiniest of the kittens hiding in a closet. If it hadn't been for her, it would have died!" Maggie Rose responded urgently.

"Wow, that's fantastic." Furry Face held me to his face again. "You're amazing, Lily! We're going to get along just great."

Maggie Rose's shoulders drooped.

"And those kittens are pretty cute," Furry Face went on. "I think, though, that a puppy is maybe all I can handle for now. But I was serious, Mrs. Murphy—come on my show. Help people understand that abandoned and lost animals need our help."

"Thank you, Johnny. I'll be in touch. Say good-bye to Lily, honey," Mom replied.

The sadness coming off my girl was so strong it was suffocating. Furry Face held me out, and Maggie Rose gathered me to her, tears flowing freely down her face. "Good-bye, Lily. I love you," she whispered. Then her sobs burst out into the open.

"Hey, hey, what's this?" Furry Face asked with concern. "Why are you crying, Maggie Rose?"

"She's just having trouble getting used to parting with our animals," Mom said.

My girl lifted her face from my fur. "Not *animals,* Mom. Lily. Lily is the only dog I have ever wanted in my whole life."

The man went very still. Then he turned and looked at Mom. "I guess I didn't understand."

Mom shook her head. "No. It's okay." She tried to put an arm around Maggie Rose, but my girl didn't hug back. "Maggie Rose is just coming to terms with something that all people in our job have to learn—that animal rescue is a constant flow," she told Furry Face. "New animals arrive at shelters every day. They get placed with foster families until we find them permanent homes. But when a foster family can't bear to give up the animal they've been taking care of and adopts it, they usually stop fostering new animals. It's a huge problem for us, because our shelter is small and we need our foster homes or we have to turn away new arrivals. So we can't keep the animals ourselves, no matter how much we love them. We have to set the right example for all the volunteers who work for us."

My girl pressed her face into my fur again.

"I understand, I guess," the man replied. "But I feel bad. Tell you what. I sort of have my heart set on this little girl, but that doesn't mean I can't share. You could come visit her any time you want. Would you like that? And maybe I could take her to see you, too. If I needed a dog sitter, I would drop her off with you, if your parents said it was okay."

Feeling Maggie Rose's pain made me want to whimper. I squirmed up so I could lick her wet face. When were we going to go home?

19

I thought my girl couldn't possibly feel sadder, but now what came off her was such a suffocating grief I could not help but whimper. Things were even worse than before! I couldn't help my girl feel better, and I seemed to be making things worse!

My girl's hands were trembling when, all of a sudden, she thrust me away from her. Now Furry Face was cradling me. *He* felt sad, too. What was wrong with me? Why couldn't I be a good puppy for all these people? And why was Maggie Rose giving me to this person when she obviously needed her dog more than ever?

Maggie Rose reached into her pocket and pulled something out. It was not a treat or anything that smelled good—it was a piece of paper.

"This is a picture I drew of Lily," she said to Furry Face. Her voice went up and down in a strange, sad way. I could tell she was using all her strength to keep from taking me back and holding me as tightly as she could.

"I wrote a poem for her under the picture," she went on. "Please, could you put it up somewhere where Lily can see it?"

Furry Face shifted me to one hand and reached out the other for Maggie Rose's paper.

"I will definitely do that," he said solemnly.

"And on the back there's something even more important," Maggie Rose told him. "There's a list of all the animals Lily has rescued."

Furry Face turned the paper over and looked at the back.

"Missy, Freddie, deer," he read out. "Five kittens. Lily's really helped all these animals?"

He looked from Mom to Maggie Rose. Mom looked confused. Maggie Rose nodded.

"When she saves more animals, please add them to the list," she said. On the last word, her voice went very thin and high and wobbly, and all of a sudden she turned and ran straight to the van. She climbed in and slammed the door behind her.

Mom turned to Furry Face and sighed. "I'm sorry. I thought it would be good for her to come here and see

Lily's new home, to meet you and know Lily will be loved. But that may not have been the right call."

"Oh, I'll give this little puppy all the love she can handle. But I guess I'm feeling torn. Are you sure about this?" Furry Face replied.

Mom shook her head. "Honestly, no, I'm not sure, not sure at all. Maggie Rose is tenderhearted and loves all the animals in the shelter. She's always been happy to help us find new homes for a puppy or a kitten or whatever. I thought it would be the same with Lily. I can't tell why this is different. Her brothers have been teasing her a lot lately. Maybe that's all it is."

"I get it," the man answered. "Well, thank you. I promise I will give Lily the best home possible, and I meant what I said. Your daughter can come here any time for a visit."

"Thank you," Mom said.

I was trying to worm my way into a position in Furry Face's arms so that I could see my girl in the van, but the way he was holding me blocked my view. Then Mom walked away, going around the back of the van. Now I couldn't see her, either.

"You'll be all right, Lily," Furry Face told me.

I was absolutely bewildered when, with a lurch, the van slid backward out into the street. Finally, I could see Maggie Rose! Even from a distance, I could tell that her face was flushed and wet with tears. I wriggled to force Furry Face to put me down so I could run to her, but he just clutched me to him. "Good dog," he murmured. He carried me up some steps and through a door, closing it behind him.

Good dog? How could I be a good dog when I wasn't with my girl?

He set me down on the floor. I went to the door, put my nose to the crack underneath it, and inhaled with deep gusts. I could barely pick up my girl's scent, but it was fading. Maggie Rose was leaving without me!

I scratched at the door so that it would open, but it didn't.

"Hey, Lily, want a ball?" the man called softly. I barely glanced down as a white ball rolled past my vision. I needed to be with Maggie Rose!

Furry Face sighed. "Hey," he said. "I know you don't get it, but you're going to be my dog now, okay? Maggie Rose can come visit you any time she likes, I promise."

I heard *Maggie Rose* and felt pretty sure he was telling me my girl would be back soon. She always came back in the mornings, didn't she? When I had to spend the night by myself, I could bear my loneliness because I knew that she would be coming back to see me in the day. She was my girl, and I was her dog.

I circled a few times and then lay down right in front of the door so that I would know the moment the van came back up the driveway.

The man went into his kitchen. Soon I could smell something delicious cooking, but I didn't budge from my post. I couldn't risk even a moment away from that door because I wanted to be sure to be there to greet my girl.

I heard Furry Face talk a little, rattle things a little, and chew a lot.

I didn't move.

"Hey, Lily. I put some food in your bowl," Furry Face said quietly.

I breathed in, searching for my girl's scent. I couldn't find it.

When the crack under the door was no longer glowing with daylight, Furry Face moved around the house. He snapped switches on the walls, and the rooms were suddenly full of brightness. It was then that a terrible thought struck me.

What if Maggie Rose wasn't coming back?

This idea was so terrible that it made me whimper. I breathed out a great gust of air at the crack between the door and the floor so that my nose could pull in a deep breath. Surely, somewhere there would be a sign of my girl. I needed Maggie Rose!

"Lily," the man said. He put his hands on my fur, and I quit crying. "I'm so sorry, girl."

I slept right there by that door that night, waking up often. I heard something drive by. Was it the van? A faint voice came to me. Was it my girl? More than once a human smell drifted in through the crack. Maggie Rose?

In the morning, Furry Face put a leash on my collar—no treat—and led me Outside. I squatted, and he forgot to give me a treat for that as well, but that was fine. I was too busy for treats. I was searching for my girl. Her scent was painted on the grass. I breathed in deeply. My girl, it was the smell of my girl.

Back in the house, I took up my position in front of the door.

"It's the weekend. What do you want to do?" the man asked me. "Go for a walk? Lily? Go for a walk? Play with the ball? Want to play with the ball, Lily?"

He was saying my name and tossing out a lot of words that I loved to hear, words like *ball* and *walk,* but I wasn't really paying attention. Any time now, I knew, Maggie Rose would be back.

He knelt by me and put his hand on my back. "Don't you believe I love you, girl? Don't you believe you'll be happy here?"

I turned my head away from him and sighed. I could tell that he was kind, but he wasn't my girl.

After a little while, Furry Face got up with a sigh of his own. He opened the door. I picked my head up alertly. Maggie Rose was coming?

No. She was not there. Furry Face went out quickly

and shut the door behind him. He was back in a minute, with a newspaper under his arm. This time, when he shut the door, it bounced back a little so that it was open a crack. Probably he did that so I could more easily sniff for my girl. I did sniff, but there was still nothing of her on the air.

I dropped my head back to my legs and let it lie there heavily. Furry Face stepped over me. "It'll take time, Lily," he said softly. "You'll get used to being here."

He walked into the kitchen and began to make interesting noises there. My ears twitched. But I couldn't go investigate because I didn't want to leave the door in case Maggie Rose came back.

I pushed my nose into the crack between the door and the floor once more to check if my girl was nearby. When I did that, the door moved into the house, widening the crack.

I pushed again. The door moved a little more.

I jumped to my feet. Furry Face was opening and shutting cupboards and putting things in bowls. Normally, this was activity that I would have been very interested in, but not now. Now I was focused on pushing at the door with all the strength in my body.

It opened! I squeezed through the crack.

Maggie Rose had not come back. Obviously, it was up to me.

I had to find my girl.

To get to her, I realized, I would have to go through a whole new Outside. I was not in the Outside that I was used to back home, the small yard where Maggie Rose and I played Bring It Here. I was not in the much bigger Outside where we'd played the same game with Sammy.

This Outside was very busy. It had sidewalks set into the grass that I could walk on, and many houses like the ones where Furry Face lived. Cars and vans went past along a wide street.

I hurried down one of the sidewalks with my nose up in the air, searching for a hint of Maggie Rose.

I could not smell her anywhere! But there were so many other smells, it made my head swim. Dirt. Grass. Trees. Flowers. Bushes with damp earth underneath that would be good for digging. Trees—some of them with broad, soft leaves and some with spiky needles and that same sharp, dreadful tang I remembered from my time playing Bring It Here with Sammy.

Other animals! I could smell them! There were dogs and cats inside some of the houses I passed. Squirrels like Sammy chittered at me from trees. Animals I had never met had walked across the grass in the night. Some of them had peed on it! I crisscrossed the grass of several lawns, my nose down to the dirt, sniffing hard. This was so interesting!

I wandered for what seemed like a long time, across many lawns and past many houses, but I couldn't find a trace of Maggie Rose. Surely, she must be somewhere—but where?

I was crossing yet another lawn when the track of a strange new animal caught my attention. It smelled wild like Sammy, and big and rather fierce. I couldn't help myself—I followed it.

The track led me behind the house and to some tall plastic bins that smelled very good indeed. Food was inside them! Delicious food, lots of kinds, all mixed together! I could even smell peanut butter in there! I scrabbled at the sides of the bin with my paws, but it didn't open up. I barked at it. That didn't work, either.

My barking did, however, attract the attention of a dog inside the house, who barked back loudly, telling me that this was his house and not mine.

Fine. I did not want to be in his house, anyway. Maggie Rose was not in there.

I crossed the lawn in back of the house, squirmed beneath a row of bushes, and trotted across a new lawn and a brick patio. I could hear something now, a familiar voice calling, "Lily! Lily!"

It was Furry Face, saying my name. I paused and sniffed the wind. I could smell him not far away.

I was supposed to go to people who said my name.

But Furry Face was not Maggie Rose. My pull toward my girl was stronger than the tug that told me I should go to Furry Face when he called me.

If only I could figure out where in this enormous Outside my girl had gotten to!

20

I headed away from Furry Face and found myself up against a fence. I sniffed along it and
found a hole where the not-dog I'd been tracking had
clearly wiggled through. I did the same and came out
on the other side of the fence into a wider, wilder Outside.

The grass was longer. There were more bushes and
trees and even a stream not too far away; I could smell
the clean wetness of the water. To my right and left, I
could see more homes and backyards, but ahead of me
was a dense, deep wildness.

So many animals lived here. I could hardly believe
what my nose was telling me. There were not-dogs
everywhere! Some were tiny insects burrowing through

the soil at my feet or dug into the bark of trees. Some were birds flitting overhead or scolding from branches. One was like a twist of shiny rope, and it uncoiled itself and slithered away beneath a stone when I came close.

I had my nose to the thick grass, sniffing hard. My girl had not walked here. Maybe I should go back under the fence and search for her some more? But it was hard to stop sniffing. There was a brand-new smell right at my feet—a new not-dog, one I had never smelled before, had hurried across this grass not long ago.

My feet followed my nose along the trail this creature had left, and I wound up against a fallen log, sniffing hard.

Something was hidden under there. Something small and frightened and alone.

It wasn't another kitten; I could tell. It was a new kind of animal. I sniffed hard and barked once. Maybe it needed to come out and play? Maybe then it would feel better?

It did not come out.

I took my nose away from the log and looked around. Did this small, frightened, furry animal have a mother nearby? Should I try to find it? Should I bring the animal to its mother, just as I'd carried the little black kitten to Maggie Rose?

Something rustled in a nearby bush. My head jerked around. Was this a mother?

No. It wasn't.

The animal that had been hiding in the bush came out slowly. It looked a little like a dog, with a black, twitching nose and alert whiskers. It looked a little like a cat, because its head was round and its ears stood straight up from its head.

But it was not a dog or a cat. It smelled wild and hungry. And I could tell that no human hand had ever petted its fur.

I knew this smell. I had smelled it in the backyard with the plastic bins and followed it through the hole in the fence. And I had smelled it before that, too— long ago, on Missy's fur.

This not-dog was not friendly. It did not want to play. It had black eyes that glittered at me inside black fur that made a mask across its face. It had a puffy tail with stripes that quivered behind it as it stalked slowly closer to me.

It wanted to get at the small, frightened creature beneath the log. I did not think that should happen. This fierce not-dog would certainly not make that small hidden thing feel better.

I felt the fur on the back of my neck bristle. I felt my lips pulling back from my teeth.

I barked as loudly as I could. I would scare off this not-dog! I would make it go away!

The not-dog paused. It shook its head as if it felt a little confused. Then it lowered that head closer to the ground. It made a grunting noise at me. Now it was my turn to shake my head. Was the thing trying to bark back?

The not-dog bunched its back legs underneath it, and suddenly it rushed at me. Startled, I leaped away. But it stopped before it got too close, and I realized that it had only been trying to scare me away from the log.

I raced back and barked more, bracing my feet wide on the earth, lowering my head. I sent a message with my barking: *Don't come any closer! Stay back!*

Far off, I heard a familiar voice calling, "Lily! Lily!" but I was too busy to answer Furry Face right now.

The not-dog backed away one or two steps, but it did not leave. Instead, it began edging to one side. It was moving in a circle, and I had to turn with it to keep facing it and barking.

It was bigger than I was. Its teeth looked very sharp, too. If it rushed at me again and did not back off, I would not be able to fight it.

But maybe it didn't know that.

I doubled my barking and added some growls. I showed all my teeth. The hair all the way along my

spine was standing up, and I had not even told it to do that! It made me look bigger and tougher. But it was too bad I could not bristle all over the way kittens did. Then I could really scare this intruder away.

Over my barking, I heard a new voice calling my name. It was not Furry Face this time. "Lily! Lily! Do you hear that barking? Lily!"

It was my girl!

I was so surprised that I quit barking. My head whipped around in my girl's direction, so fast that my ears swatted the sides of my head. Maggie Rose! I should run to her!

I took one leap in her direction, and then I whirled back to the log.

If I ran away, the not-dog would be able to get at the frightened animal under the log.

But if I didn't run to Maggie Rose, I might not be able to find her again. She might even think I did not want to be with her!

The thought made my whole body ache with my longing to be in my girl's arms. I needed to be with her. I needed to comfort her. I needed to take care of her and let her take care of me.

But if I ran away, I would be leaving the small frightened creature all alone. That couldn't be the right thing to do.

Maggie Rose loved all animals. She'd cradled the

small black kitten after I had found it. She'd petted Stripes and Blotchy. She'd worried about Freddie. She didn't love any of these animals as much as she loved me—and that was only natural, since I was her dog— but they mattered to her. She took care of them.

I had to do that, too. I had to take care of the small animal under the log.

The not-dog had sensed my hesitation. It came closer with its mouth wide open and all its teeth on display. It let out its breath in a huffing sound that I think was its way of trying to growl.

I put my head down and growled right back, as loud and fierce as I could be.

"Lily!" cried my girl's voice, louder than before. I heard running footsteps crunching on old leaves and soft earth, and suddenly, there she was! My girl! She pushed through a tall bush, shielding her face with her arms to keep it from getting scratched, and hurried right to me.

The not-dog took one look at her and ran off, rustling through tall grass. I dashed to my girl as Mom and Dad and Furry Face came pushing through the bush as well.

I jumped up at Maggie Rose's knees, wagging my tail as hard as I could. My girl! I'd found her!

She scooped me up and held me close and kissed me. I kissed her back, licking her cheeks and neck and ears and as much of her as I could reach. It had been so long since I'd seen her!

"Did you see that raccoon? Lily was barking at it!" Maggie Rose said, holding me close.

"I just caught a glimpse of it, yes," Mom said.

"It looked like a young one to me, probably not even a year old yet," Dad added. "That's lucky! A big, full-grown raccoon might have gone after Lily. They can be aggressive, and she's just a puppy."

Maggie Rose held me even closer. "Lily, Lily, I'm so glad we found you," she whispered.

"Funny that the raccoon was out in daylight," Dad went on. "They're nocturnal. Maybe this one got lost. She'll be in big trouble with her mother for wandering around in the daytime, I bet!" He smiled at Maggie Rose and patted me.

I wiggled around to lick his hand and wag at Furry Face and Mom. It was nice to have all my friends here with me.

"What were you doing here, though, Lily, huh?" Maggie Rose asked me. "You shouldn't have been in the woods at all."

"I must have left the door unlatched when I came back from getting the paper," Furry Face said. "I do that a lot. Guess I'll have to adjust my habits." He came over to pet me, too. I liked getting attention from so many people at once.

"It's a long way for such a little puppy to come," Mom said. "I wonder what brought her to the woods." She was looking thoughtful, and she left us to walk over to the log where the tiny, frightened creature was hiding.

That reminded me that I still had something to do. I wiggled until Maggie Rose set me down, and then I hurried over to the log and stuck my nose into the hole where the small not-dog was hiding.

It was still just as scared. I pawed at the dirt and yipped once to let the creature know that everything was safe now. It could come out and play. Then I looked up at Maggie Rose. Since she was here now, she'd make everything all right.

Mom bent down and looked in the hole. "Oh," she said, very softly.

She took hold of my collar and pulled me back. Then she picked me up and handed me to Maggie Rose.

I squirmed to get down, but Mom shook her head. "Hold on to her," she said to Maggie Rose, still softly, and she drew all the humans several steps away from the fallen log.

"Is there something under there?" Furry Face asked. He seemed to understand that he was supposed to speak softly, too.

Mom nodded. "Look!" she whispered.

A tiny, twitching nose was poking out of the hole under the log. A smooth little head followed, with two long ears that quivered with the slightest sound. The creature crawled out of the hole, and I could see that it was no larger than Sammy.

A new friend to play with! But Maggie Rose did not understand how much I wanted to play with this tiny thing. She held me firmly, and I couldn't get down.

The creature looked around with wide dark eyes, stared at us for a moment, and then darted away. In a moment, it had vanished in the long grass.

And I didn't even get to play Chase Me!

"A rabbit," Maggie Rose whispered. "Just a baby one!"

Mom nodded. "That's right. I bet it just left its mother. It probably hasn't been on its own for more than a few days."

"Lily was protecting it!" Maggie Rose said. "She saved it from the raccoon!"

"Lily to the rescue," Furry Face said softly. He patted me again.

Mom smiled. "Well, even a little rabbit like that could outrun a raccoon if it needed to. But it was so young—it probably didn't know what to do, so it just went to ground."

My girl buried her face in my fur. "Lily, you're the best," she whispered to me.

"Thanks for coming so quickly to help me look for her," Furry Face said to Mom and Dad. "I didn't know who else to call."

"We're very glad you did call us," Mom said. "It's what we do. And now . . ."

She put a hand gently on Maggie Rose's shoulder. Maggie Rose looked at her, and I felt the same old sadness rise like a massive force inside my girl.

"Let's go back to Mr. Mancuso's house, hon," Mom said gently.

"Yes," said Furry Face suddenly. He was looking hard at Maggie Rose. "We should go back there."

Maggie Rose nodded miserably. I squirmed around to lick under her chin. Usually that made her giggle, but it was of no use now.

"You'll need Lily's leash. And that picture you drew of her, with the list on the back," Furry Face went on. "You'll need to add the baby rabbit to the list of animals Lily has rescued. When you take her home with you."

Hope spiked inside my girl, and my head snapped up. Something had happened to change how she felt. But what?

"Johnny," Mom said to Furry Face. "I'm not sure I understand what you mean . . ."

"Lily missed you so much," Furry Face told my girl. "She cried by the front door all night. I think we may need to reconsider some things here."

My girl was trembling just a little. I looked around alertly, in case I needed to scare off any not-dogs who might be frightening her, but I couldn't see or smell any.

"I don't want you to feel that you have to . . . ," Mom said hesitantly to Furry Face.

"Lily's a rescue dog," Maggie Rose said, with her eyes on Mom. "She saves animals. Like Dad does. Like you, Mom. I know you have a rule, and I know all the reasons about foster failure—I know! I do! But Lily's special. She's not just any puppy. She could work at the rescue. She could really help there. I think that's what she's supposed to do."

"It's almost like Lily belongs to the rescue as well as to Maggie Rose," Dad said quietly. "But I meant it, Chelsea. I will support whatever you decide."

Furry Face and Mom and Dad looked at one another. My girl tucked her face into my fur. She was breathing quickly.

Mom turned to both of us. "Maggie Rose," she said, "I am so sorry for what I've put you through. I think I was focused on the wrong things. You're right. Lily has an amazing knack for bonding with other animals. And more importantly, she's yours. Lily is your dog now."

And with that, the sadness that had been lurking inside my girl for such a long time left her completely. "Yes! Yes! Lily, you're my dog!" she whispered. "Lily! Lily! Lily!"

I barked, loving her giggles. I wiggled until she was forced to set me down, and I raced in circles at her feet, so thrilled with this change of mood that I didn't know

what to do with myself. There were no bouncy toys to be found, but I located a stick and pounced on it and shook it and dashed back and forth, hoping someone would do Chase Me in celebration.

"Wow, look at all that energy." Furry Face laughed. He turned to Mom. "Maybe Maggie Rose is right. Maybe I should start with a cat."

"We can arrange that," Mom replied. "In fact, we just got some in."

Maggie Rose dropped to her knees and spread her arms, and I abandoned the stick and ran to her. She wrapped me in a hug. "You're my dog now, Lily. You belong to *me*," she whispered happily.

I didn't know what she was saying, but I knew this: I was her puppy, and she was my girl, and finally, finally, I had made her happy.

Reading & Activity Guide to
Lily's Story: A Puppy Tale
By W. Bruce Cameron

Ages 8–12; Grades 3–7

Synopsis

It's love at first sight when animal-loving Maggie Rose meets rescued pit bull mix puppy Lily, at the animal shelter where Maggie Rose's mother works. In *Lily's Story: A Puppy Tale,* by W. Bruce Cameron, these two little sisters (one human, one canine) prove that their big hearts matter more than their size, birth order, or breed. In their respective human and puppy families, big brothers teach them the challenges and rewards of "sibling-hood." At the shelter and off-site, Maggie Rose and Lily learn important lessons about pet and wildlife rescue from Maggie Rose's animal-shelter-president mother and game-warden father. And they learn a lot about each other, too. Maggie Rose discovers that Lily, though she herself is a rescue animal, has the heart and temperament to help other animals in distress. And Lily learns that making "her girl" Maggie Rose happy—whether that means bonding with "non-dogs" at the animal shelter, distracting a wild deer, or just playing ball—is the most fulfilling job of all. In spite of obstacles and separations, Maggie Rose and Lily find a way to stay together and show everyone that, once in a while, a "foster failure" can be a true success!

Reading *Lily's Story: A Puppy Tale* with Your Children

Pre-Reading Discussion Questions

1. In *Lily's Story: A Puppy Tale,* canine narrator Lily's mother is a pit bull. Pit bull-type dogs have received a lot of "bad press" for being dangerous, but they also have many advocates who challenge the negative stereotypes. Have you heard or read good or bad things about pit bulls? Do you have a particular reaction to a dog when you know (or find out that) it is a pit bull, versus another kind of dog? Is this reaction positive or negative? Why?

2. Lily is rescued and brought to a shelter as a puppy. Have you ever visited an animal shelter, or fostered or adopted an animal from a shelter? What did you learn from that experience?

3. The story's human main character Maggie Rose learns a lot about animals from her parents, since her mom is president of the Colorado animal shelter where Lily the puppy comes to stay, and her dad is a game warden. Can you think of other jobs related to wild animals or pets? What are the jobs? What do you know, or would you like to learn, about these jobs?

Post-Reading Discussion Questions

1. In Chapter 1, pit bull puppy Lily and her mother and brothers have been rescued and brought to a shelter. Shelter president Chelsea Murphy's children—Craig, Bryan, and Maggie Rose—come for a visit. How does Lily being the only girl, and the "runt" (or smallest, weakest puppy) in her litter contribute to the special bond she develops with Maggie Rose?

2. In Chapter 2, Maggie Rose introduces Lily to some of the other animals at the shelter and explains: "That's what we do, Lily. We find families for animals who don't have homes. Like you!" Why is this important work? What might happen to stray, homeless, or abandoned animals if rescue shelter workers didn't find and help them?

3. Lily meets Missy, a lost Yorkie who has a raccoon bite on her leg. How does Lily help Missy? When Lily sees Missy reunited with her owner, she observes: "In that instant I understood something new. My life here in this place with my mother and my big heavy brothers was a good life, but it was not what a dog needed most. To be truly happy, a dog needed to be like Missy and have a person of her own." Do you think this is true for your own dog, if you have one, or of a friend or relative's dog you have observed?

4. What does Maggie Rose's mother explain about the concept of a "foster failure" in Chapter 4, when Maggie Rose says she wants to adopt Lily? Does this change how Maggie Rose feels about adopting Lily? How does Maggie Rose prove, over the course of the story, that Lily should be an exception to the rule about shelter workers (and their families) not adopting pets from the shelter?

5. What do you think about Maggie Rose's choice to hide Lily in her shirt when potential adopters come to visit the puppies, in Chapter 5? If you were in Maggie Rose's situation, would you do the same thing? Why or why not? When the family interested in adopting one of Lily's brothers expresses concern about pit bulls being dangerous, what does Maggie Rose's mother explain to them? What are some of the misconceptions about pit bulls she clears up?

6. In Chapter 6, when Maggie Rose's middle brother Bryan tries a harsh training approach with Lily, Maggie Rose says:

"Mom says that kids at school are always picking on you, and that's why you pick on me. And it's not fair." Have you experienced, or talked about, situations with bullies? Do you think bullying sometimes is a cycle, in which bullies feel insecure so they pick on, or put down, others so they will feel better about themselves? What do Bryan and Maggie Rose learn about each other in this scene, which starts with the heated argument and ends with Bryan giving Maggie Rose the personal journal?

7. Maggie Rose and Lily go with Maggie Rose's father (who is a game warden) to release Sammy the Squirrel back into the wild, in Chapter 7. How does using pine cones to "play catch" with Sammy the Squirrel help Lily finally master the "Bring it here" command Maggie Rose has been trying to teach her? When Maggie Rose and her dad return from releasing Sammy, her dad hears Maggie Rose's oldest brother Craig call his sister a "runt" What do we learn about how Dad feels about this nickname, and how the term relates to Maggie Rose's relationship with Lily?

8. When another family might adopt Lily, Maggie Rose's parents discuss what to do. Maggie Rose's mom feels she needs to follow her own rule that shelter workers (and their families) cannot adopt animals. Maggie Rose's dad sees his wife's point of view, but sympathizes with his daughter, too. If you were Maggie Rose's parents, what would you do in this situation? What are some of the extra considerations for Maggie Rose's mom, since she has to look at the decision from both work and family perspectives?

9. In Chapter 10, Maggie Rose's dad invites her to survey a mountain goat herd at Echo Lake, so she won't be at the shelter when the new family visits Lily. Maggie Rose sneaks Lily into a cat carrier and brings her along. Do you think

Maggie Rose makes the right choice to do this? Why or why not? How does Lily help rescue the deer trapped in wire fencing, when Lily's dad receives the call from the sheriff's department?

10. In Chapter 12, Lily observes that a new man who comes to meet her "wore fur on his face." What are some of your favorite examples from the story of humorous observations and descriptions Lily shares from her puppy point of view?

11. Maggie Rose wants to keep Lily because she loves her and thinks they belong together, but she also thinks Lily can play an important role at the shelter. Maggie Rose tells Lily: "We're going to try something new. I'll prove to them that you're meant to be a rescue dog." How does Lily prove her skills as a rescue dog in her interactions with kittens Blotchy and Stripes, and Freddie the Ferret?

12. Maggie Rose and her mother are bringing Lily to her new owner (radio disc jockey Johnny Mancuso) when her mom gets a call to rescue some kittens that have been found in an empty apartment. How does Lily help with the rescue? How does she discover and save a kitten the people would have missed?

13. What is the list on the back of the picture and poem, which Maggie Rose gives to Lily's new owner, Johnny? What does Lily do at her new owner's home to show how much she misses Maggie Rose?

14. In the final chapter, Lily picks up the scent of a small, frightened creature hidden under a fallen log, and tries to protect it from an unfriendly raccoon. Why doesn't Lily leave the little creature under the log even when she hears Johnny, Maggie Rose, and Maggie Rose's parents calling for her?

15. After reading the story, do you agree with Maggie Rose that Lily is not just a *rescued* dog, but also a rescue dog? What

did *Lily's Story: A Puppy Tale* teach you about the important role people (and sometimes other animals) can play in helping scared, hurt, and homeless animals?

Post-Reading Activities
Take the story from the page to the pavement with these fun and inspiring activities for the dog lovers in your family.

1. **Bullys, Not Bullies!**
   National Pit Bull Awareness Day (NPBAD) was established to increase understanding and appreciation of bully breed dogs, generically known as pit bulls, and to dispel some of the negative stereotypes surrounding this group of dogs. You can check out www.nationalpitbullawarenessday.org to learn more about this positive public relations campaign for the pit bull. Together with your child, gather art supplies, such as poster board, construction paper, markers, paint, crayons or colored pencils, and other decorative elements. Then, work as a team (or invite friends and family members to join you) to design and create posters for National Pit Bull Awareness Day. What images and messages can you include on the poster to help educate people about the positive qualities of pit bull-type dogs, and to correct or clarify some of the myths, or misinformation, about them? National Pit Bull Awareness Day takes place each October. You might save your poster for that dedicated day, or choose to hang your poster (with permission) in school or community venues throughout the year.

2. **Silly Lily Pet Portraits**
   Animal rescue officer Joan Simmons, who works with Maggie Rose's father and Lily to rescue the wild deer, calls the rescue pup "Silly Lily." Keeping this nickname in mind, in-

vite your child to revisit the text and try to visualize some of the funny interactions Lily has with other animals throughout the story. Provide paper, paint, and colored pencils, and ask your child to sketch, draw, or paint his or her vision of a favorite interaction or scene. Subjects to consider might be: Lily's interactions with her mother dog, her older brothers, other shelter pets, such as Poppy, Brewster, Oscar, Freddie the Ferret, Sammy the Squirrel, Missy, the lost Yorkie, Stripes and Blotchy, the shelter kittens; or the kittens Lily helps rescue from the vacant apartment; or the baby bunny she protects from the unfriendly raccoon. You might invite friends or family members who have read *Lily's Story: A Puppy Tale* to do their own Silly Lily portraits; or they can do paintings or drawings of silly moments featuring their own pets. If desired, arrange an art show where everyone displays and shares their work. Perhaps you can invite other friends and family to the art show, asking guests to bring an optional donation of dog food, toys, or other supplies, which you can donate to a local animal shelter or rescue.

3. **How Can You Help?**

Animal shelters often have minimum age requirements for on-site volunteers, but there are lots of ways you and your child can support the important work shelters do to help homeless, hurt, and abandoned animals. Together with your child, do online research to find out about local shelters or rescue organizations in your area, then contact or visit the shelters to see if you and your child can make animal treats, toys, or blankets to donate to the pets at the shelter.

Reading *Lily's Story: A Puppy Tale* in Your Classroom

These Common Core-aligned writing activities may be used in conjunction with the pre- and post-reading discussion questions above.

1. **Point of View**

   Lily has an earnest, friendly voice as the story's narrator. Looking at the world through her "furry filter" offers a curious, humorous puppy point of view. Ask students to pick a key scene from the story and write 2–3 paragraphs using the point of view of another animal or human character (such as Freddie the Ferret, Sammy the Squirrel, one of Lily's brothers; or, Maggie Rose, shelter worker Amelia, or one of Maggie Rose's parents or brothers). Remind students to consider how author W. Bruce Cameron uses humor, details, and sensory-rich description to make Lily's voice authentic and unique, as they develop a believable, compelling voice for the character they select.

2. **Fingerprints and Paw Prints**

   From the outset of the story, author W. Bruce Cameron highlights similarities between human and puppy protagonists Maggie Rose and Lily. Invite your students to identify and explore, in a one-page essay, parallels that can be drawn between these two characters. Students should include relevant examples, quotes, and details from the text, and make inferences from characters' dialogue, actions, or interactions. (Students might consider aspects such as, the characters' roles in their families; interactions with siblings; feelings about their size and status; special connection with each other; the desire and ability to help animals; ways they contribute at the shelter.)

3. **Text Type: Opinion Piece**

   Maggie Rose wants to adopt Lily from the animal shelter, but her mom says no, telling Maggie Rose: "one of the first things I did when I started working here was to make a strict rule. Staff and volunteers can't adopt any animals from this shelter at all." Do you agree or disagree with this rule? Why? If you were president of an animal shelter, would you have this rule at your shelter or not? Ask students to explain and defend their opinion in a one-page essay. Invite them to use evidence from the text, or additional research (if needed) to support their position.

4. **Text Type: Narrative**

   Ask students to write 1–3 pages in the voice of Lily's mother, telling the story of how this mama pit bull and her puppies come to the shelter. Draw on details from the text, and your imagination, to describe what it was like to keep your puppies safe before being rescued. Where were you living before you came to the shelter? What was it like to arrive at, and adjust to, the shelter? How did you feel about interacting with shelter workers and volunteers for the first time, and seeing them interact with your puppies? What were you thinking, feeling, seeing, smelling, hearing, and tasting in this new environment? How did it make you feel when visitors started coming to meet, and adopt, your puppies? How did it feel to get adopted yourself, and have to leave Lily alone in the kennel?

5. **Research & Present: This Is Pit!**

   The main character in *Lily's Story: A Puppy Tale* is loyal, loving rescue pup Lily. Her father is an unknown breed and her mother is a pit bull. Pit bulls are a type of dog, not a specific breed. The term pit bull can apply to a range of purebred and mixed breed dogs, such as the Staffordshire bull terrier, American pit bull terrier (APBT), American Bulldog, or American Staffordshire terrier. Invite students to do online and library research into one of these breeds or mixed breeds, or an aspect of pit bull-type dogs, such as history, (including involvement in bear and bull baiting and dog fighting), physical attributes and temperament, negative media attention, breed-specific legislation, or positive public relations efforts, such as the National Pit Bull Awareness Campaign. (**HINT:** Check out www.blessthebullys.com). Have students present their findings in a PowerPoint or other multimedia style presentation.

6. **Research & Present: Animal Rescue Work**
   In Lily's Story: A Dog's Puppy Tale, readers learn about careers in the area of animal rescue. Maggie Rose's mother is the president of an animal shelter, while her father is a game warden. Have students work in pairs or small groups, to research a specific job in animal welfare and rescue (such as Conservation Officer, Environmental Scientist, Ecologist, Fisheries Technician, Park Ranger, Wildlife Biologist, Animal Shelter Manager, Pet Adoption Counselor, or Veterinary Technician). (**HINT:** Check out gamewarden .org, or animalhumanesociety.org for more animal-related career options and information.) Have students organize and present their research findings in an oral presentation, supported by colorful visual and written aids.

Supports English Language Arts Common Core Writing Standards: W.3.1, 3.2, 3.3, 3.7; W.4.1, 4.2, 4.3, 4.7; W.5.1, 5.2, 5.3, 5.7; W.6.2, 6.3, 6.7; W.7.2, 7.3, 7.7

About the Author

W. BRUCE CAMERON is the *New York Times* best-selling author of *A Dog's Purpose, A Dog's Journey, A Dog's Way Home,* and the young-reader novels *Ellie's Story, Bailey's Story, Molly's Story, Max's Story, Shelby's Story,* and *Toby's Story.* He lives in California.

Introducing
LILY TO
THE RESCUE,

a brand-new chapter book
series from bestselling author

W. BRUCE
CAMERON

Don't miss these heartwarming stories
about a rescue dog who rescues other
animals! Charming illustrations
throughout each book bring Lily and her
rescue adventures to life.

STARSCAPE

BruceCameronBooks.com

W. BRUCE CAMERON

LILY TO THE RESCUE

Cover Not Final

W. BRUCE CAMERON

LILY TO THE RESCUE

TWO LITTLE PIGGIES

Cover Not Final

Available 3.17.20